CLOSE ENEMIES

President Kissonga of mineral rich
Rezengiland has recently been ousted and
replaced by President Mani Saiki. Amid talk
that the new regime will nationalise the
mines, the SOD's team, Alex and Charlie
are tasked with the protection of the new
president, armed with the knowledge that
MI6 thinks that corruption is rife even in
the new regime. Alex and Charlie get to the
bottom of it – but it's a close run thing.

CLOSE ENEMIES

Close Enemies

by

Nick Curtis

Dales Large Print Books
Long Preston, North Yorkshire,
BD23 4ND, England.

British Library Cataloguing in Publication Data.

Curtis, Nick
    Close enemies.

    A catalogue record of this book is
    available from the British Library

    ISBN   978-1-84262-769-3 pbk

Published in Large Print 2010 by arrangement with
Working Partners Two

Dales Large Print is an imprint of Library Magna Books Ltd.

Printed and bound in Great Britain by
T.J. (International) Ltd., Cornwall, PL28 8RW

With Special Thanks to Graham Edwards

For Helen

Prologue

June 4th

09:04

Grand Hotel, Limpopo City

Like all writers, Jack McClintock had a muse. Some muses spoke through dreams, others whispered on the wind. Some, he gathered, were like angels. Jack McClintock's muse was a little different. She clocked in at nine and delivered hard-boiled copy to order. Like Jack, she got paid by the word.

From the chipboard desk where his laptop rested, Jack stared out onto the balcony of his shabby fourth-floor hotel room. *The Times* wasn't stretching the expense budget for him on this trip, and accordingly his muse was slow to descend. Turning back towards his computer he typed:

The presidential cavalcade drove out of the dawn to cross the bridge over the Limpopo River.

He took a mouthful of strong coffee and

9

read back what he'd written. Hardly inspired prose. He hit the delete key. Maybe the problem was that the events he was trying to describe hadn't happened yet. That was the trouble when you got paid by the word. You liked to get as much in the bank as possible before breakfast. Jack yawned and scratched his incipient beard: there was no one to impress in this backwater.

He stood up from the uncomfortable seat, stretched and paced over to the doors opening on to the narrow balcony. He didn't go too close: the metal parts of the rail were pitted with rust and the wooden parts had disappeared completely. It was sad. In its day, the Grand Hotel must have been truly opulent, a colonial jewel gleaming in its African setting. Not any more. The whole place wore a dejected air. The marble colonnades were grimed with traffic fumes, half the statues had been spirited away, the high ceilings of the lobby and restaurants sagged.

Was the restoration of decaying colonial heaps high on the new President's agenda? It didn't seem likely.

Still, it was good to stand here and look out across the river. The hotel had a commanding position overlooking the Saiki Bridge. The bridge crossed the Limpopo

River at its narrowest point, just before the river turned on to the eastward course that would lead it, after much meandering, to the Mozambique border. On the far side was the Presidential Palace, a curious mix of Middle-Eastern domes and gothic spires. An untidy rear wing and a baroque fountain completed the mess. The Republic of Limpopo had shaken off colonial rule way back in 1965 and, since then, a succession of presidents had indulged some rather eccentric ideas about architecture. *Power*, Jack pondered, *is no guarantee of taste.*

The street running in front of the hotel was still fairly quiet – just a few people on bicycles or in battered pick-ups, bringing their crops to market. Jack doubted the change of president would affect them much.

Certainly, the new name for the river crossing hadn't yet caught on with the locals. Up until a few weeks ago, it had been called the Kissonga Bridge. But the former President Kissonga was now licking his wounds in – if the rumours were true – neighbouring Botswana. The new regime under Mani Saiki had stepped in with much pomp and ceremony. The renaming of the bridge was typical of the changes so far: all but costless and completely superficial.

Jack could hardly claim to be an expert in Limpopo politics, but the press focus on the recent election and a day spent reading through the archives had brought him up to speed. When his editor had painted a too-good-to-be-true picture of an unspoilt sub-Saharan paradise, he'd known for sure it was a bum assignment.

But Jack – and his muse – went where they were told. Besides, since he'd landed in Africa, his hay fever hadn't troubled him at all.

The decaying hotel summed up the state of the whole country. Kissonga had been a tyrant who loved bureaucracy. As a result, he'd turned the country's constitution into a nightmare of red tape. Nothing ever got done. The only channels he'd kept clear were those that enabled him to indulge his favourite hobbies: the illegal trafficking of automatic weapons, diamonds and ivory. There were plenty of people – both in the Republic of Limpopo and in international circles – who were glad to see Kissonga go.

There were also some who were not so pleased.

Returning to his laptop, Jack tried again.

In the dawn light, the cavalcade drove out from the Presidential Palace to cross the

Limpopo River via the newly rechristened Saiki Bridge. Security was tight, with the presidential limousine surrounded by police cars and motorcycle outriders. Despite his confident inaugural address last week, Mani Saiki is as cautious now as when he first came to power.

President Saiki's destination this morning was the government assembly hall in downtown Limpopo City. In his opening address, he outlined a series of sweeping changes to the Republic of Limpopo's constitution, changes so radical they would see one third of the current bureaucracy removed in a single blow. Not for Mani Saiki the mire of officialdom, bequeathed to him by ex-President Kissonga. Saiki wants the world to believe he is a man ready to roll up his sleeves and get things done.

The telephone on his bedside table jangled like an angry alarm clock. Christ, when was the last time he'd heard a phone with an actual bell inside it? On the third ring, he snatched up the receiver.

'This is Hector,' said a hoarse voice. 'You might want to look through your window.'

With a soft click, the line went dead.

Jack had met Hector – if that was his real name – in the hotel bar the previous night. Hector worked in the Presidential Palace kitchen. In exchange for an evening's worth

13

of heavily-iced whisky sodas, he'd promised Jack a heads-up when things got interesting.

He went back to the window. Sure enough, a cavalcade of vehicles was proceeding in stately fashion out of the palace gates. The powerful African sun turned their windscreens gold.

The cars snaked away from the palace. It was all happening just the way he'd written it. The only difference was that it wasn't dawn. Jack forgave himself the indulgence; even rent-a-muses got poetic occasionally.

The quality of the light was magical all the same: the sun was still low enough to toss long shadows off the palace towers, through the dusty air, out across the river. The black cars crawled like beetles along the hard-packed road, tyres squirting up runnels of sandy grit.

At the head of the procession was a cluster of small police vehicles. They churned towards the bridge with every light ablaze: headlamps, hazards, roof-arrays. Behind the police cars were two black Mercedes, followed by the big presidential Rolls. On each wing of the Rolls waved a Republic of Limpopo flag; the windows were tinted as black as the paintwork. Following were two smaller limos and yet more police cars. Just as Jack had imagined, a flurry of motorcycle outriders kept the whole thing tightly buttoned.

As the cars started across the bridge, a grey-haired man in the street on Jack's side of the bridge dropped his bike to the ground and started jumping up and down on the spot, arms waving wildly in the air. Jack smiled and wondered how he could write the old geezer into his article.

When the presidential limousine reached the central span, the Saiki Bridge exploded.

The bomb went off directly under the Rolls. The President's car rose into the air on a cloud of dust and concrete shards; a second later, the sound of the explosion hit Jack's ears. Beneath the disintegrating Rolls, the bridge deck broke away from its supporting tower. Metal reinforcing rods sprang like giant piano wires out of the road, one after the other.

The blast threw one of the trailing limos sideways. It slewed into the line of outriders, knocking men and bikes through the disintegrating parapet and down into the river. The car stopped with its rear end hanging in space, back wheels spinning wildly. The Rolls had slammed on to its roof, scattering glass across the road.

The cars at the head of the procession

screeched on their brakes; from every door burst policemen and black-suited security officers. Most pulled guns from holsters, ready to protect their President. Others dived for cover behind their vehicles as debris from the explosion rained down on them. Jack saw a giant of a man shouting wildly into a walkie-talkie shortly before being crushed beneath a falling chunk of concrete the size of a domestic fridge.

Seconds later, the bridge's central span folded up completely. The presidential Rolls slid on its roof across the collapsing pile of metal and masonry. Then it was in empty space, plummeting nose-first into the swollen brown waters of the Limpopo. When it hit, it threw up a curtain of spray. Yellow foam gushed over the exposed chassis as the current tumbled it downstream to an area of quieter water. It bobbed for a few seconds more, like a child's toy, before sinking slowly beneath the waves.

Small fragments of concrete continued to patter down on to the surface of the river. Survivors crept out from their hiding places. Jack could hear their distant shouts as they wandered around in bewilderment and staggered to the torn edges of what had once been the Saiki Bridge.

I wonder what they'll call it next, he thought.

The men peered down into the water in search of their comrades. Their President. On the near shore, the old man with the bike was just standing there, hands wrapped tight into his grey hair.

Jack McClintock smiled and shook his head. It looked like the copy he'd be emailing to his editor this morning wouldn't end up tucked away on page five.

Suddenly he was writing front page news.

Jack sat down again at his laptop and highlighted everything he'd written so far, and pressed delete.

How's the muse going to spin this one? he wondered.

1

June 19th

12:45

SOD Headquarters, New Scotland Yard

Charlie Paddon wiped the sweat from his brow and entered the meeting room. Fifteen minutes late: not exactly clever, but it could have been worse. The traffic round Whitehall had been heavier than he'd expected and a car could go only so fast through the streets of London. Even a red BMW with an officer of Special Operations – Diplomats behind the wheel.

He just hoped he hadn't missed the lunch.

Everyone looked up as he made his way round the table to the one remaining empty seat. The room was hot, the air clammy. Charlie's boss, Chief Superintendent Brian Burfield, grunted a vague greeting; the only other person to remark was the thin man

18

sitting opposite Brian.

'So glad you could join us, Chief Inspector Paddon,' said Nick Luard with an unconvincing smile. 'I hope that little red car of yours hasn't been giving you trouble?'

'Good afternoon, Nick. Not at all. My meeting at Downing Street over-ran, I'm afraid. You know how the PM is when it comes to security issues. I did explain the head of MI6 was waiting, but he was having none of it.'

Luard's smile turned to a scowl. 'Perhaps we can get on now,' he muttered.

Charlie took his seat next to his partner, Alex Chappell. As he sat down, she gave him a smile as warm as Luard's was chilly.

'Trouble?' she murmured.

'No,' he whispered back. 'Downing Street want to change a few of their shift patterns. Just keeping us informed. As routine as it gets.'

'So that's why Brian didn't want to go.'

'Why be the organ grinder if you can't send your monkey?'

'You know you've got sweat-stains on your shirt?'

'Can I help it if it's muggy as hell out there?'

'Not much better in here.'

19

A newspaper skidded across the table and landed in front of Charlie.

'When you two have finished,' Brian said, 'take a look at the front page of *The Times*.'

Actually Charlie had already seen it – in the waiting room at Downing Street. But he scanned it again anyway. The headline read: 'Security fears as Republic of Limpopo President visits UK'.

The article – an exclusive by Jack McClintock – began with a recap on the big story from a couple of weeks ago: the failed attempt on President Saiki's life, during which not he but his decoy had been killed. There was a picture of the President inspecting the ruins of the bridge, with a small inset showing the wrecked Rolls Royce being dragged from the river. Speculating on whether Saiki would be safe in London, McClintock wrote, 'If British Special Operations do not take this visit seriously, the next river crossing to be blown up may well be Westminster Bridge.'

Typical McClintock. But what struck Charlie as he reread the article was the number of column inches devoted to the African mining industry – in particular, to a South African mining magnate called Piet Bakker.

'Bakker,' the article asserted, 'was a regular

dinner guest of the Republic of Limpopo's former President Kissonga. During Kissonga's lengthy term of office, Bakker Diamonds and Minerals opened no fewer than six new mines – two diamond and four cobalt – within the Republic. Sources suggest that President Kissonga would not have granted Bakker exclusive mining rights unless there were some advantage to be gained for his government, or himself personally. These rumoured exchanges became known as "Bakker-handers".'

Set into the text was a picture of a glowering Bakker. He looked remarkably like a pit-bull terrier.

So far so McClintock. His next claim, however, was more startling: that the corruption extended beyond the borders of the Republic of Limpopo. All the way to the United Kingdom, in fact. Not only had Piet Bakker been siphoning company profits to give cash bungs to Kissonga (and this was where McClintock's phrasing became artfully vague), but Bakker and Kissonga had also enjoyed the benefit of an alleged 'British connection' that had allowed 'millions of Limpopo Rennits' to 'pour out of the country'.

It was what Charlie thought of as 'tightrope

journalism': every sentence carefully balanced so as not to attract a lawsuit. He could just imagine *The Times* legal department going through McClintock's copy with a fine-tooth comb. Still, it wasn't like McClintock to go out on a limb unless he knew something.

'He doesn't quite say Bakker's a crook,' said Charlie, sliding the paper back across the table. 'But he comes pretty close.'

'Bakker *is* a crook,' said Brian. He loosened his tie, unbuttoned his collar and managed to look generally dishevelled. Summer heatwaves didn't suit the head of Protection Command. 'Everyone knows that. Just look at him. Give him a twin, you'd call him a Kray.'

'If you ask me, Jack McClintock's playing a dangerous game,' said Nick Luard. In contrast to Brian, he looked as crisp as a just-tossed salad. 'If I were his editor, I'd have advised him not to open his mouth until he was in full possession of the facts.'

'And I suppose you *are* in possession of the facts?' said Brian, without looking up from the newspaper.

Luard said nothing, just smiled.

'Corrupt or not, the fact of the matter is Piet Bakker's a dinosaur,' said the grey-haired man at the head of the table. As secretary to the Security and Intelligence Coordinator, it was Henry Worthington's job to make sure Brian Burfield and Nick Luard didn't rip each other's heads off. It wasn't always easy. 'For thirty years he's plundered the region's mineral resources and nobody has batted an eyelid. The Republic of Limpopo is just another pie he's got his fingers in. And this man has an awful lot of fingers. But times are changing. He thrived during the apartheid years but right now, what with all the other changes going on in South Africa, he's beginning to look very exposed.'

'Not before time,' said Alex, looking up from her own set of papers. 'This report says his mines have a poor safety record. I bet his workforce wouldn't be sorry to see him go.'

'He's still one of South Africa's biggest employers,' countered Luard, 'which is why they continue to tolerate him, even today.'

'You sound as if you approve,' said Alex. Charlie, hearing the rising tone in her voice, kicked her ankle gently under the table. Her anger was righteous, but it wouldn't do to upset the head of MI6.

Before tempers got too heated, Henry

Worthington stepped in.

'This debate is all very interesting,' he said, 'but if we could return to the matter in hand. We are here to discuss next week's visit by the President of, in particular the security issues it raises. Brian, you're in charge of the SODs' – Brian raised his eyebrows at this – 'it's your policemen who'll be out on the streets, making sure the President is safe while he's on British soil. Would you like to kick things off?'

'I'll pass that buck straight to Charlie, if that's all right, Henry,' said Brian. 'Like you say, he'll be the one on the ground. Charlie – first impressions?'

'Well,' said Charlie, 'obviously my main concern is the recent assassination attempt. I was wondering if MI6 could bring us up to date on their intelligence regarding the incident?'

All eyes turned to Nick Luard. *If he was a bird,* thought Charlie, *he would start preening about now.*

'As we know,' Luard began, 'President Saiki felt nervous enough that morning to put one of his aides in the presidential Rolls and himself in one of the other vehicles. Whether he knows who actually planted the bomb, however, is still open to speculation.'

'Care to speculate then?' said Brian Bur-field, rolling his eyes.

'It's true the international community has broadly welcomed Saiki's rise to power. But there are still plenty who'd like to see him fail. Remember, the previous administration under Kissonga had built a very big, very cosy nest for itself. Saiki's started tearing the whole thing apart. He's bound to be ruffling a few feathers.'

'As usual,' said Brian, 'you're telling us what we already know. Have you got any-thing resembling a list of suspects?'

'Kissonga had a lot of friends.' Luard waved his hand vaguely. 'The list could be very long indeed.'

'That'll be a "no" then,' Brian muttered.

Charlie felt Alex tensing beside him. She got frustrated when Brian and Luard bickered. 'They want their heads banging together,' she usually said after meetings like this. He tapped her ankle again.

At the head of the table, Henry cleared his throat.

'While security is clearly our primary con-cern here today, I would like to remind everyone that, politically, President Saiki's visit is an enormously significant one. In just a few weeks, Mani Saiki has become something of an international celebrity. Yes, we have to keep him safe, but we also have to keep him in the spotlight. The eyes of the world are on us. Saiki has come to represent the changes sweeping through all of Africa. He is, of course, as interested in his country's mineral resources as Kissonga was, but with one critical difference: Saiki wants to see those resources exploited fairly, in ways that benefit his people. He has no time for the likes of Piet Bakker. That's why he's coming here. He's keen to forge new links with British industry that will safeguard his country's prosperity for years to come.'

'Very rousing, Henry,' said Brian. 'I just hope he's not disappointed. Africa's still a battleground, and it's hardly jolly hockey sticks over here. We're talking diamond mines after all. People get very ... *excited* about diamonds.'

'Actually,' said Henry, 'I understand it's the cobalt that's taken over. They use it in mobile phone batteries, apparently. But I take your point. That's one reason Saiki's appointed a new Minister for Minerals.' Henry shuffled through his briefing sheets. 'Paul Malamba. He'll be on the plane with Saiki. A bright chap by all accounts – forty-five years old, bags of experience in the mining industry.

The hope is Malamba will bring some real-world knowledge to the whole political process. It should make for an interesting mix.'

Charlie flipped through the duplicate sheets on the table in front of him. On the third page was a short biography of Malamba. It seemed that before his appointment to Saiki's government, Malamba had been General Manager of Bakker Diamonds and Minerals in the Republic of Limpopo...

Bakker again. The name jumped off the page. *With Kissonga gone and Saiki in power, Piet Bakker suddenly has a lot to lose. Saiki must know that. So why rock the boat by hiring Bakker's right-hand man?*

Charlie tapped the name with his finger and raised his eyebrows at Alex.

'How's your maths?' whispered Alex. Charlie suppressed a smile. It was their code for 'something doesn't add up'.

Reading on, he noted with interest that Malamba had been educated in England – York University to be precise. He was about to remark on this when Henry Worthington pre-empted him.

'President Saiki's agenda is of course very full. But he's already indicated to us that Malamba is keen to catch up with some of his old university chums. It's about twenty years since he was here and he wants to make up for lost time. Oh, and they're both keen to do some shopping.'

Charlie exchanged another glance with Alex. He knew exactly hat she was thinking.

Two weeks ago the man was nearly blown to smithereens. Now he wants to hit Selfridges!

'Have you advised him of the security risk that poses?' he said.

Henry shrugged. 'The president insists.'

2

June 19th

13:10

SODs Headquarters, New Scotland Yard

Lunch arrived on plastic platters wrapped in cling film. Henry gave a silent groan. Another flatfoot feast. The pork pie was the worst. You could say what you liked about Whitehall – at least the catering was top-notch.

Still, the appearance of the food meant they could get down to the nitty-gritty. In Henry's experience, these kinds of meeting were like parties: the best bits always happened in the kitchen. Or, in this case, around the big table at the far end of the meeting room.

'Usual caterers, Brian?' he said as they made their way to the table.

'No,' said Burfield. 'It's a new outfit. Opened up just round the corner. We thought we'd try them out.'

To Henry's surprise – and delight – the platters were packed with fresh seafood, sumptuous quiches and pastries so light they were practically transparent.

'Not bad,' he said, piling his plate as high as decorum permitted. 'I hope your budget can take it.'

They stood and ate and watched the sun melt the tarmac on the road outside. All the windows were open but the air was thick and still – didn't they have air conditioning in this place? It amused Henry to see that Burfield and Luard were nursing their plates at opposite ends of the table. In contrast, Charlie Paddon and Alex Chappell stayed close. When Paddon wasn't looking, the woman stole food from his plate.

Paddon broke the silence.

'It's curious,' he said. 'I know President Saiki's the main event and given the assassination attempt we'll have to be extra vigilant – but I can't help thinking this visit is really all about Paul Malamba. What do you think, Henry?'

Reluctantly, Henry took his eyes off the quiche. 'I think you're right,' he said. 'I see you've been reading the sub-text.'

'Well,' Paddon replied, 'I don't know

about sub-text. I just know there's more to all this than meets the eye.'

'Isn't there always?' muttered Brian Burfield. He was already filling his plate with seconds.

'Well,' said Henry, 'what the briefing sheets don't go into is the American connection.'

'There's an American connection?' said Alex.

'Like I said,' said Burfield, 'isn't there always?'

'You'll be aware,' Henry continued, 'of the rumours surrounding the elections that brought Saiki to power? That the CIA ... shall we say *assisted* ... in the counting of votes?'

'You're saying the Americans rigged the election?' said Paddon.

'I wouldn't go that far. Although the Republic of Limpopo does have a history of corrupt electoral practices, there's no doubt about that. How else could Kissonga have stayed in power for so long?'

'Mandela's visit in '97,' said Burfield, seizing the apple turnover Henry had been hoping to snaffle. 'That was the turning point. That famous picture of Mandela sharing the platform with the Republic of Limpopo Congress Party. The second he did that, Kissonga's days were numbered. Clinging on to power for the last decade was remarkable.'

'Quite,' said Henry. 'However, even if the CIA was involved, its only interest will have been to ensure a fair ballot. My point is, the Americans have made it clear they're right behind Mani Saiki and the RCP. It's hardly surprising: they're keen to make friends with as many people as they can in sub-Saharan Africa. Remember those two terrorist training camps that turned up in the region last year? The Americans feel that, what with all those plateaux tucked away in its interior, the Republic of Limpopo could be the perfect breeding ground for the next generation of suicide bombers.'

'I suppose their sudden interest has got nothing to do with all those diamond and cobalt mines?' said Paddon. Chappell and Burfield both nodded vigorously. Even Nick Luard, on his own near the rye-bread bites, allowed himself a thin smile. 'I mean,' Paddon went on, 'ensuring a "fair" election is one thing, but it's something else when what you're really after is a big pile of shiny stones.'

'Don't underestimate the appeal of shiny stones,' said Chappell.

'Anyway,' said Henry, gritting his teeth, 'the fact is the Americans *are* interested in

Limpopo, and in Paul Malamba in particular.'

'Why him?' said Alex.

'Because he wants to nationalise the mines. That means severing ties with South Africa. In particular with Piet Bakker. As far as President Saiki's concerned, that will allow the Republic of Limpopo to stand on its own two feet. As far as the Americans are concerned, it will make the Republic a country they can do business with.'

'It goes further than that,' put in Luard. 'The Americans *adore* Malamba – he's practically a poster boy. He's had at least two write-ups in *Time* and if he achieves everything he wants to achieve on this visit I guarantee there'll be a script going round Hollywood within the year. They'll probably cast Denzel Washington in the lead.'

Paddon nodded. 'And the shiny stones are just of passing interest. I wonder,' he went on before Henry could interrupt, 'why the Americans are so keen to jump into bed with Malamba? It says quite clearly in the briefing sheets he used to be Piet Bakker's General Manager. You've got to ask why he's so ready to stab his former employer in the back.'

It was good, Henry supposed, to employ policemen with brains. But sometimes he just wished they'd just stand in a corner and say, 'Yes, sir'.

'Nick,' he said, 'why don't you share what you've uncovered about Paul Malamba's special relationship with Piet Bakker?'

'Thank you, Henry,' said Luard, dabbing his mouth with a napkin. 'In fact, I've prepared a little presentation on the subject. If you'll bear with me.'

Luard brought his laptop over from the meeting table. While he was waking it up, Henry was able to dart in and take the last slice of quiche. To compensate for the lost apple turnover, he treated himself to a chocolate brownie.

'Want me to get a projector?' said Burfield as Luard wedged the laptop between two plates of sandwiches.

'I doubt your kit's compatible,' said Luard. 'MI6 hasn't used sixteen-millimetre film for years.'

'Ha ha.'

They gathered round the screen and Luard punched up the first of his slides. It showed an open cast mine. Dumper trucks swarmed on its slopes like ants servicing the nest.

'My God,' said Alex. 'It's huge.'

'It's even bigger than it looks,' said Luard.

'Those look like regular trucks but they're not – the wheels alone are bigger than a Land Rover. This is the Katseru diamond mine, just inside the southern border of the Republic of Limpopo. At the time this photograph was taken – that's nine years ago – Katseru was the third largest of its kind in the world.'

'Run by Bakker?' asked Charlie.

'Of course. This is where Paul Malamba spent twenty years of his working life. For all that time he was a loyal employee of Bakker Diamonds and Minerals. He rose quickly through the ranks, gained Bakker's trust and – more to the point – kept it right up to the day he resigned. No mean feat, given Bakker's reputation.'

'Bad?' said Charlie.

'Piet Bakker treats people just like he treats the minerals he takes from the ground – as resources to be exploited. Malamba's very different – a people person. They're chalk and cheese, which might explain why they worked so well together. What's less easy to explain is why Malamba stayed on after the explosion.'

'What explosion?' asked Alex.

Luard clicked through to the next slide. It was another photo of the mine, this one taken from the floor of the gigantic excavation. In the background was a heap of wreckage that might once have been a vehicle. In the foreground was a sign reading: NO UNAUTHORISED ACCESS.

'Nine years ago there was a serious safety lapse at Katseru. Are any of you familiar with the kinds of blasting procedures they have in these mines?'

'Why don't you refresh our memories?' said Henry. He wished Luard wouldn't make these things feel like the first day at school.

'They use something called ANFO – that's a mixture of ammonium nitrate and fuel oil. The ANFO is mixed on location in a specially equipped truck and pumped directly into a series of holes bored into the ground. The holes are lined with plastic to stop the explosive leaking out. They fit detonator caps, then run wires from the caps out to a safe location. When the site is clear, they blow the boreholes in rapid sequence. Most of the charge is directed underground – it's like an earthquake. After that they send in the excavators and start digging. On this occasion, something went wrong.'

The next slide was grainy black and white, obviously taken with a telephoto lens. It showed more wreckage, including countless shredded tyres. Lined up on the ground beside the wreckage, covered in sacks, were what could only have been human bodies.

'Standard procedure is to use a single lorry with a crew of three to mix the ANFO. The lorry works its way along the line of boreholes, filling each one in turn and capping it off. For some reason – presumably to speed up the whole process – Bakker started using six lorries at once.'

The picture changed again. It was the same picture as before, in close up. Sticking out from beneath one of the sacks was the unmistakeable shape of a human hand.

'That's eighteen men handling high explosive simultaneously. Not actually as dangerous as it sounds, but add to that the fact that less then half of them were trained, and add to *that* the fact that they started running out the wires to the detonator before the ANFO teams had finished their operation...'

'I think we can guess the rest,' said Paddon.

The final slide showed another wide view of the mine. In the foreground was a truck carrying not rocks but corpses.

'Thirteen people died, including three members of Paul Malamba's family, who were working at the mine: his older brother and two cousins. Officially, it was an accident. Malamba was off-duty at the time.'

'Where did you get the pictures?' said Burfield. 'Was MI6 there? Was Bakker under investigation?'

'Not personally. But, yes, MI6 was ... well, let's just say we were in the area.'

'In the area? What does that mean?'

'We suspected one of Bakker's directors of running an arms racket on the side. We'd had surveillance in place at Katseru for a number of months. As well as gathering evidence for our own investigation, we also learned that the Bakker approach to health and safety was what you might call "lackadaisical". This particular incident was a perfect demonstration of the kind of short-cuts they were taking. The lapses were occasional – and usually happened when reliable types like Malamba were off-site – but when they did happen they were serious. And we have evidence to suggest the board of directors knew exactly what was going on.'

'But you didn't do anything about it,' muttered Burfield.

'Not our remit,' said Luard, scowling at the Chief Superintendent. 'Our brief was to crack the arms racket – believe me, that was a much bigger deal. We couldn't afford to jeopardise our prime objective by kicking up a lot of unnecessary dust. But we leaked what information we could. Spread rumours. Over recent years Bakker's procedures have improved immensely. I'd like to think we helped things along.'

'What about Malamba?' said Paddon. 'Do you think he knew about these rumours? I mean, he worked with these people. He must have suspected something.'

'I'm sure he did,' Henry agreed. 'Which puts a rather different complexion on things, don't you think?'

'I'm amazed Malamba didn't kick up a fuss,' said Alex. 'Or resign at least. I'd have gone ballistic.'

'I agree,' said Henry. 'But I think Paul Malamba is cleverer than that. What would he achieve by resigning? I think he's spent the last nine years playing a waiting game, advancing his political career to the point where he can hit Piet Bakker where it hurts. That's what his nationalisation proposal is all about. He wants to take Bakker's business away, lock, stock and barrel. You know what they say: "Revenge is a dish best served cold."'

'Nobody will cheer for Bakker if Malamba

manages to take him down,' said Burfield. 'But you can bet he'll put up a fight.'

'Probably. But Bakker knows nothing about the nationalisation plans. Not yet, anyway.'

'As soon as he does, he'll be on the war-path.'

While they all thought about this, Henry poured himself a glass of orange juice. It was time they got back round the table. They still had Mani Saiki's itinerary to go through, plus all the rest of the detail work necessary to make sure the president's visit went smoothly and securely.

It's all in the preparation, he thought, putting down his glass and his empty plate. *Cover the bases now and we're less likely to be surprised later.*

Taking his lead, the others stacked their empties on the table. He imagined a small mob of policemen gathered outside, hungry for the leftovers. The only person who didn't move was Nick Luard.

'Shall we reconvene, Nick?' said Henry. 'There's a lot still to get through.'

'Without wanting to throw the cat among the pigeons,' said Luard, watching serenely as the others seated themselves again, 'I have to point out that the story I've just

40

presented you with is actually a load of old cobblers.'

Henry blinked. You could always trust an MI6 man to pull the rug out from under your feet. And why did Luard have to look so smug while he was doing it?

'What are you talking about, Nick?' he asked.

'Oh, I don't mean the accident and the revenge idea. All that's real enough. I mean how everyone seems to think Malamba's the golden boy – especially the CIA. I don't agree. He's a long way from squeaky clean and he certainly isn't the movie hero the Americans would have us believe. If you ask me, there's a lot more to Paul Malamba than meets the eye.'

3

June 24th

09:15

Highway 2, Republic of Limpopo

Paul Malamba checked his Rolex. The plane wasn't due to leave for nearly an hour. Plenty of time to enjoy the ride. And plan the future.

Clouds of dust rose behind the black Mercedes as it followed the river towards Limpopo International Airport. The road was well-paved, but the west winds still brought in enough Kalahari dust to hide an army of elephants. Malamba caressed the crocodile skin of his attaché case and gazed out of the window.

Limpopo International Airport. What a joke.

For now, at least, it was true. The airport had one runway and a passenger terminal that looked like an American roadside diner. The baggage handling facility was a shed with a conveyor belt ripped out of an old shoe factory. Worst of all, the only scheduled flights were to OTR Tambo in Johannesburg. Going through South Africa was a small inconvenience, but a significant one: leaving the yard was getting easier by the day, but you still had to use the neighbour's gate.

Not for much longer.

The airport, just coming into view through the sun-soaked dust, was already showing signs of change. Rising from the plain was the skeleton of the half-finished international terminal. Beside it sat the new control tower, a space-age marvel of steel and glass. The tower contained practically enough technology to direct the traffic over JFK or Heathrow. Overdesigned it might have been, but its presence was a conscious statement of ambition.

'You looking at the new tower, too, sir?' said James, his driver. 'Me, I think she looks like a piece on that chessboard of yours.'

'She does,' said Malamba. 'The queen.'

'Don't see no more planes through, sir.' James turned and smiled, revealing a row of huge, glossy teeth.

'That will change. Next year Limpopo Airways will be flying into Zambia and Botswana. And that is just the start. Give it a few years, James, and nobody will have to go through South Africa at all. Instead, everyone will be coming through the Republic of Limpopo.'

James laughed. 'And there's me thinking you're just the Minister for Minerals. Next you'll want to be president yourself!'

The car was approaching a grove of acacia trees.

'Slow down, James,' said Malamba, tapping on the glass partition separating them.

'Whatever you say, sir,' came the cheerful reply.

The Mercedes coasted past the trees. Filling the branches were the interlocking nests of colony weavers. Each tree was home to thousands of birds. Some were sagging under the weight of the nests. It was a beautiful sight, wholly African – just the kind of thing the tourists loved. Perfect position too: halfway between the airport and the city.

We should build a car park and a lodge. I must mention it to the Minister for Tourism when I see him next.

'Thank you, James,' he said, tapping the glass again. 'You can put your foot down now.'

But the Mercedes didn't speed up. In fact, it slowed even more. Malamba leaned forward in his seat, suddenly apprehensive.

'What is it, James?' he said.

'Traffic, sir. Plenty of it. No worries though. We've got lots of time before you catch your plane. And that pilot, he won't dare start his engines until the president gets on board!'

The road ahead was packed with vehicles: cars and mud-spattered pick-ups, a handful of bigger trucks, all jammed bumper-to-bumper, crawling along. Malamba stared morosely at the queue, then peered through the back window.

'Can you see President Saiki's limousine?' he said.

In the mirror, James smiled. 'No worries, sir. The president's car, she's got Samuel at the wheel. He'll be sure to stay two miles behind us, all the way, whatever happens. And the decoy – she's two miles ahead. Bubba's driving her. Bubba, he knows what he's doing. So take it easy. Even if somebody tries to blow us up, the president will be perfectly safe!'

'It wasn't the president's safety I was thinking about,' said Malamba, under his breath.

He closed his eyes, tried to relax. His Mercedes was unmarked, but it was still big and black and shiny. An attractive target for anyone with a grudge against the new regime. That was the trouble with bombs: as soon as one went off, everybody assumed it was open season. He started grinding his teeth.

In one of his typically overblown election speeches, Mani Saiki had likened the corrupt Kissonga administration to an ocean clogged with pack ice. The Republic of Limpopo Congress Party, he elaborated, was the ice-breaker, come to cut through decades of stagnation.

It was not a bad metaphor. Especially if you saw Saiki as the ice-breaker's sharp prow. The blade you could dispose of as soon as its work was done.

This was how Malamba had thought of Saiki all the way through the campaign: disposable. Someone to take the spotlight while others worked behind the scenes. Someone to catch the eye. Above all, someone who could bow out when the understudy was fed up of waiting in the wings.

The failure of the assassination attempt was a mixed blessing. Saiki had lived, but the close call seemed to make him more manic than ever. Still, now the dust had settled, Malamba was beginning to believe he would be better off with Mani Saiki alive.

Without Saiki, it would be harder to push through Malamba's own long fought-for policies – in particular, his plans to nationalise the mines. Saiki was nothing if not energetic. That was already proving good for the country: the Republic of Limpopo was buzzing. Perhaps it would be good to keep him in office for a while. For all his faults, the man was proving quite a success.

Success, however, always came at a price, and in this case it was payable in US dollars.

Just a few nights earlier, Malamba had been unable to sleep through worry about this debt. His wife, Alice, had woken at two in the morning to find him sitting bolt upright in bed. 'You should be happy, honey,' she'd said, gathering him up and holding him close. As always, he felt safe in her vast expanse. She was a big woman in every way. 'You won.'

'But we could not have done it without the Americans. This is what Saiki does not understand. Our so-called independence is only an illusion. When will we stand on our own two feet?'

'Be patient. Use those feet to take one step at a time. Let that be enough for now.'

Her words were well-meant – and she was right, he knew it. But it did not still his concern. 'Uncle Sam may have a big smile on his face,' he said, staring into the darkness outside the window, 'but the chalice he offers is poisoned. If you are friendly with the United States you attract some extreme enemies. Enemies who like to make their point with high explosives.' He turned in her arms. 'Violence begets violence. What if someone plants a bomb under *our* car? What if you and the children are in the car?'

'That is why we keep our house a long way from the city. All will be well, my Paul. All will be well.'

The next day, Malamba had returned from his home in the foothills to the little apartment he kept in Limpopo City. At least this way Alice and the children were safe. Still, he hated being apart from them.

All the more reason to put his plans into action. If doing that meant holding an American hand, so be it. In fact, he would do almost anything to see his dream come true.

But what about Mani Saiki?

Long term, he was probably more of a hindrance than a help. That was fine by Malamba: he did not believe Saiki had staying power. The president claimed he could run a marathon but, like most politicians, he was strictly a short-distance operator. Given time, the man would simply fall by the roadside, exhausted.

Paul Malamba, on the other hand, was playing the long game. With so much on his agenda, what other game was there to play? Change was everywhere, on the wind, like the Kalahari dust. Time for him to change, too. No more waiting in the wings. There were so many new opportunities to seize.

There was too much to do.

The Mercedes was making steady progress. The traffic was bad, but at least it was moving. After ten minutes they reached the cause of the hold-up – a battered VW microbus, the side of which boasted (in shaky sign-writing): LIMPOPO ARPORT SHUTEL.

The VW was half in the ditch with two of its tyres blown out. The passengers had spilled on to the road and were trying to heave it upright. They looked remarkably cheerful.

Not exactly what we want the tourists to see, thought Malamba, as they passed the broken-down bus and got back up to speed. Then he smiled. The half-baked taxi firm was just another example of free enterprise at work. Limpopo City had seen more new businesses start up in the past two weeks than in the whole of the past two years. You had to be happy.

'Sir,' said James, as they neared the airport, 'I was wondering – when you go to London, will you be visiting the embassy?'

'Of course, James,' said Malamba. He was fascinated by the sleek lines of the new control tower, the way the light poured down it like water.

Keeping one hand on the wheel, James slid back the glass partition and squeezed his other hand through. Dangling from it was a small gold crucifix on a chain.

'What is this?' said Malamba.

'It's for my brother. He works in the embassy. Security. We play games, we two, on the internet. We keep score and when I win he sends me a prize and when he wins I send him a prize. So last week he won. This here, that's just something I picked up in the River Road market. Isn't nothing special, but I just hate to put it in an envelope, you know what I mean?'

Malamba took the crucifix. 'What game do you play?' he asked, quietly.

'Oh, mostly poker, maybe a little black-jack. Why d'you ask?'

'No reason.'

'So ... will you do it, sir? I know it's mighty impertinent, but...'

'It is no problem,' said Malamba, folding the crucifix into his pocket. 'Trust me – I will make sure this is delivered safely. What is your brother's name?'

'Toby, sir.'

The road reached the airport perimeter fence and turned to follow the line of the runway. As they sped past the chain-link, an old Dakota lumbered out of the sky to land right beside them. The aircraft's skin was the same red ochre as the earth. Its fat tyres hit the tarmac with an outraged squeal.

The Dakota stayed with them until the fence turned them away from the runway and towards the passenger terminal. As the limousine eased into one of the privileged parking bays, Malamba clicked open his attaché case and leafed through the papers he had brought to read on the plane.

What would Piet Bakker give to see the contents of these folders?

He wondered idly how good Bakker's intelligence was. The old bastard employed spies, everyone knew that, but Malamba had been careful. Very careful. The nationalisation programme outlined in these documents was designed to fall on Bakker Diamonds and Minerals like a hammer blow. To work properly, it had to fall fast and hard. And completely out of the blue.

And if Bakker refused to lie down and give in ... well, there were other tools than hammers that could be used.

A shadow fell across the rear window of the Mercedes. Malamba snapped the case shut and clutched it to his chest. Heart hammering, he watched helplessly as someone tugged open the door and thrust a meaty hand inside the car.

'If you would accompany me, sir,' said a deep voice. 'I will escort you to your aircraft.'

With a sigh of relief, Malamba stepped out of the car and into the shadow of an enormous soldier. The man was dressed in the uniform of the Republic of Limpopo National Guard and looked as hard as his voice was soft. One hand was pointing to a sleek, silver jet parked a hundred yards away on the apron. The other was holding a sub-machine gun.

'May I take your case, sir?' said the guard.

'No,' said Malamba. 'I prefer to keep it with me.'

They made their way across the dusty concrete. Just then, the shabby Dakota appeared from behind the presidential jet, on its way to the small cargo terminal at the far end of the field. The contrast between the two aircraft was striking. To Malamba's right, a man was using a pair of paddles to guide a little blue Cessna towards a hangar. To his left, a group of passengers huddled beside a baggage train, waiting to board the next scheduled flight to Johannesburg.

Like a chess piece, he thought, remembering what James had said. He turned his driver's crucifix over in his pocket, suddenly struck by an image of the entire airport as a game board, with all the pieces in play.

He gazed over the shining silver fuselage of the presidential jet, up into the sky.

Above the African plain, above the billowing dust, above the distant riverside trees and the far, high bulge of the Mokatse Plateau, storm clouds were gathering.

4

June 25th

14:12

St James's Street, London

'I feel like one of the sentries outside Buck House,' said Charlie. 'All I need is a bearskin on my head and the tourists would be queuing up to take my picture.'

'Until you smiled,' said Alex. 'Then they'd all run away screaming.'

'Thanks for that.'

They were standing on either side of the entrance to The Cigar Box. The gilt-edged sign in the little shop window promised *The Finest Tobacco From All Corners Of The Globe.* Even if he'd smoked, Charlie doubted he could have afforded even their cheapest box of cigars.

They'd followed Mani Saiki here from the Hotel Charles Darwin on the other side of Green Park. It hadn't been so much a police escort as a sustained sprint. Given the heat-wave, that was no joke. Now the Republic of Limpopo president was inside the shop, stocking up on his favourite Dominican cigars, while his SODs protectors stood guard at the door.

'I wonder where he'll go next,' said Charlie, peering in through the glass. He could just make out Saiki's compact form. It looked like he was trying to haggle with the man behind the counter.

'If he wants to buy underwear,' said Alex, 'you're on your own.'

Charlie was about to make a quip when he realised Alex wasn't smiling. Come to think of it, she'd been humour-free most of the day. The firm line of her mouth told him this wasn't the time to ask what was wrong.

He held his tongue, clasped his hands behind his back and rocked on his heels, just like English policemen were supposed to.

Twenty minutes earlier, they'd been in the Charles Darwin discussing staffing levels with the hotel's head of security, Dave Rodriguez. As they pored over the latest schedules, President Saiki had erupted from his suite and bustled over to the lift. Charlie had caught up with him as he punched the call button.

'Excuse me, sir,' he said. 'Is there anywhere you'd like us to take you?'

Saiki spun on his heel and showed his teeth. Small and round, he resembled nothing so much as a bowling ball. *A bowling ball piling down the lane on its way to a strike,* thought Charlie. *Not something you want to get in the way of.*

'Thank you, officer,' Saiki said. His English was better than most Englishmen's. 'I should prefer to take myself.'

'I'm afraid we can't allow you to do that, sir,' said Alex, joining them. 'We have to come with you.'

Saiki gave a little bow. 'For a woman as beautiful as yourself, I will do anything. But in return you must do something for me.'

Alex threw Charlie an exasperated look. 'What's that, sir?' she said.

'Try to keep up!'

In the short time they'd been his escort, they'd got used to Mani Saiki's irrepressible energy. As he led them across Green Park, he told them how, as a young man, he'd run marathons.

'People tell me my body is the wrong shape for such pursuits, but I say success has nothing to do with bodies and everything to do with minds. In that philosophy I include both Albert Einstein and Marilyn Monroe. It may surprise you to learn I have been compared to both. And in other respects I am very like your Margaret Thatcher,' he added, as he strode out into the Piccadilly traffic. Taxi drivers glowered at the two SODs officers as they ushered the president across the road.

'Really?' said Charlie when they reached the safety of the opposite kerb. He didn't know which was more tiring: Saiki's walking pace or his conversation. 'How?'

'Each night, I sleep for only four hours. Ah, the cigar emporium is down there. I have crossed the busy road unnecessarily. Come, let us retrace our steps.'

St James's Street was relatively quiet. When they reached the shop, Alex wanted to accompany Saiki inside. Charlie convinced her to let the president go alone.

'The poor sod needs a bit of space,' he said. 'And I know this place: there's no back door. We've got it covered.'

'Plus, this way you get rid of him for half an hour.'

'That's an added bonus.' He smiled, but there was still something forced about the banter. Maybe she'd got out of bed the wrong side. 'It just makes sense staying out here. We're better placed to spot trouble.'

They settled into position, book-ending the doorway. People strolled past in T-shirts and shorts. Hot as it was, Charlie felt more comfortable in his bullet-proof vest. At least his shirt had short sleeves.

'Are you expecting any?' asked Alex, after a while. 'Trouble, I mean.'

Charlie shrugged. 'Let's hope not. But the way this guy prances around he may as well paint a target on his chest. I'll feel better when he's safely back in his suite, where we can keep a proper...'

He trailed off. A motorbike had just turned in off Piccadilly. It was a Honda 250, ridden by a skinny man in red leathers and a black helmet. The bike was moving fast, but slowed as it drew near. It was weaving slightly from side to side.

'It's just a courier,' said Alex. But there was tension in her voice that made Charlie edge his hand towards the Glock 17 hand-gun on his hip.

Back in March, they'd spent a frantic twenty-four hours chasing a Honda just like this from one end of the country to the other. Only the man riding it was no despatch rider: he was a Serbian assassin on a mission to kill the Croatian Foreign Minister. They'd averted disaster – just – but neither had looked at motorbikes in quite the same way since

As the courier drew level with Charlie and Alex, he turned his head towards them. Nothing was visible through his tinted visor. He crawled past then, with a twist of his throttle, accelerated back into the traffic. Seconds later, he was round the corner and out of sight.

'Anything?' said Alex.

'I'm not sure,' said Charlie.

The shop door crashed open. But it was just the President of the Republic of Limpopo, emerging triumphant with a carrier bag in each hand, grinning.

'Did you find what you were looking for?' asked Charlie. He couldn't help smiling, too – there was something infectious about the little man's gung-ho manner.

'In abundance! Two boxes of Ghurkha Ancient Warrior. However, I have decided that all Englishmen are afflicted by madness, if they are willing to pay such prices to the retail trade. When I return to the Republic of Limpopo, I will close all the mines and tell my people to plant tobacco, which we will sell to the English at an outrageous profit.'

'That wouldn't be fair on the Cubans,'

Charlie laughed. 'They haven't got diamonds to fall back on when the tobacco crop fails.'

'Do you think we should be fair on the Cubans, Officer?' queried Saiki. His grin hadn't faltered, but something in his eyes told Charlie he'd overstepped the mark. Or maybe it was just smugness. Pride was a complicated thing, Charlie was discovering. The Republic of Limpopo might not be one of the largest countries in the world but, like its diminutive president, it had a big personality.

With all those minerals at his fingertips, he can afford to feel superior. What he can't afford to be is complacent.

Just as he thought this, the skinny despatch rider came round the corner again.

The bike was describing exactly the same route as before. It must have gone round the block. Charlie found himself looking into the same tinted visor, searching for a face. This time he got as far as unclipping the gun.

He stepped out on to the pavement, moving in front of Saiki. Without instruction, Alex did the same. The president rummaged in his bags, seemingly oblivious to the unfolding drama.

When the despatch rider drew level with

them, he stopped.

Charlie kept his eyes on the rider and let his fingers close around the Glock's grip.

A red-gloved hand slid back the tinted visor, revealing an acne-spotted face straight out of a school playground. A ratty moustache was the only clue that this was in fact, a grown man.

'Er, d'you know where Little James Street is then?' said the courier. 'Only it's my first day and I'm really screwing this up.'

'Back there,' said Charlie, pointing. 'You went straight past it. There's scaffolding on the corner so the sign's obscured.'

The relief on the courier's face looked authentic enough. Charlie relaxed his hand. The movement drew the youth's eyes, which widened when he saw the gun.

'Look,' he gulped. 'Er, I'd best be going. Late already. Sorry to, er ... sorry.'

'Take it easy,' said Charlie, as the courier pulled down his visor and swung round into the traffic.

'Talk about policemen looking younger,' said Alex. 'He was barely out of nappies.'

'Do you wish to detain me here all day, officers?' said Saiki. Realising he'd been fenced in by his minders, he was jabbing at Charlie's arm.

'Not at all, sir,' said Charlie, smoothly. He stepped aside. 'Just keeping alert for pickpockets. We wouldn't want those expensive cigars of yours to go astray.'

Saiki clutched his bags to his chest and looked nervously around. 'I think it is a good idea for me to return to my hotel. There I can deposit my purchases in the safe. Will you please remind me in which direction we need to walk?'

Charlie ushered Saiki out into the street.

'This way, Mr President.'

After another breakneck walk across Green Park, Charlie delivered Mani Saiki back to the Hotel Charles Darwin. By the time he got to his suite, the president was rubbing his eyes.

'Jet lag,' he explained cheerily. 'I will sleep for fifteen minutes before I begin work on my speech. Tomorrow I must say clever words to important people. I need to rest before I can write them down. No doubt I will see you later, officer.'

'No doubt, sir,' said Charlie.

Just fifteen minutes to recover from jet lag, he thought as the lift took him back down to reception. *He even yawns with gusto.*

Alex was waiting for him in the car. He'd parked the red BMW in the narrow street opposite the hotel's main entrance. Even though it was in the shade, the interior was like an oven. He climbed in, fiddled with the seat and stretched.

A knot of people emerged from the hotel entrance. Charlie sat upright and reached for the door handle. But the group appeared to be free of visiting foreign dignitaries.

'I think they're with the conference crowd on the second floor,' said Alex. 'Here to discuss water purifiers or something.'

'Going out on the town, more like,' said Charlie.

They watched the water people head off towards the underground, then settled back into their seats.

Out of the corner of his eye, Charlie watched Alex. She was fiddling with the fabric on the corner of the seat.

'He's a funny little man,' she said, at last. 'I mean, he doesn't give two hoots whether someone blows him up or not, but tell him they might nick his cigars and he's jumping at shadows. And why hasn't he brought his own security people? Poor Dave's going spare in there.'

'He's a president,' said Charlie. 'He's allowed to do whatever he likes.'

'Isn't he the lucky one?' she said, with

more vehemence than normal.

He swivelled to face her. 'All right. What's it all about?'

'I don't know what you mean.'

'Yes, you do. The long face? The general sense-of-humour failure? Something's up.'

For a minute he thought she was going to cry. Her eyes glistened and her neck turned pink. Instead, to his surprise, she laughed. It lit up her face.

'Actually, nothing's wrong,' she said. 'Everything's right, I suppose. It's just ... well, I wasn't sure how I was going to tell you.'

'Tell me what?'

'Well, it's just that Lawrie – you know he's been working in Aberdeen recently – well, he's been having a lot of meetings with Bob, his boss and Abel – that's Abel Horwitz, the finance director – and, well, the upshot is Lawrie's just been offered a position in Dubai.'

Oh, is that all? 'Dubai? Sounds exciting. How long would he be gone?'

She dropped her eyes. 'Well, that's the thing. It's permanent. Lochavon Industries are setting up a new research division out there. Trans-continental pipelines, something like that. Bob wants Lawrie to make it happen. He'd be setting it up practically from scratch. Once he'd got it up to speed he'd be running the whole show. It's an incredible opportunity for him. For us.'

'You'd go out there with him?' Charlie's stomach felt suddenly heavy.

'Of course. We'd all go. I'm his wife, Charlie, in case you'd forgotten. And if we're going to do it there won't be a better time. Fraser's only two, so it's not as if we have to worry about moving schools or anything.'

'I see. Is that what you want?'

Long lashes dropped over green eyes. 'Everyone says it's a fantastic career move for Lawrie. Abel Horwitz is right behind it, although to be perfectly honest the guy's a creep, so that doesn't count for much. But I was talking to Mary – Mary Chen, in HR? She's a real sweetheart. You know those successful career women who somehow manage to stay human? She's one of those. She's based in their Canary Wharf office so we meet up for lunch occasionally. She's single – come to think of it, didn't I give you her number?'

'I thought the name rang a bell. The year you played matchmaker. First you tried to hook me up with the nanny, then you started working your way through the lunch club.'

'I arranged dozens of dates for you,

Charlie. You didn't go on a single one.'

'I like to choose for myself So what did this Mary Chen say?'

Alex pouted. 'She says he should go for it.' Charlie opened his mouth, but nothing came out. She regarded him with solemn green eyes. 'Say something, Charlie.'

'Sounds like it's all sorted. What is there to say?'

Alex lifted her hand from her lap, as if she were about to reach over to him. But she checked herself. He looked away, stared across the road at the hotel again, willing something to happen to get him out of this conversation.

'Anyway,' said Alex with a sigh, 'nothing's decided yet. We only heard at the weekend and ... well, there's a lot to discuss. There's my career to consider, too.'

But you've already considered that, haven't you? thought Charlie. *You wouldn't have brought it up if it wasn't a done deal.*

He tried to imagine Alex sitting in a strange car in a strange land, with a different partner at her side. The image came all too clearly, and he didn't like it. He'd seen enough change in the last eighteen months: first his promotion from the Met to the Diplomatic Protection Group, swiftly followed by the merger that turned the DPG into Special Operations – Diplomats. Now, to top it all, his partner was leaving the country.

He swallowed hard. 'I hope it all works out for you, Alex,' he said. 'Lawrie deserves his success. You both do. You've got to seize the day, take the chance while you can. You'll only regret it if you don't.'

'What did you do – swallow a plate of fortune cookies?' And, just like that, the old Alex was back. 'Anyway, now you've got a steady girlfriend, I figure it's safe to leave you alone.'

'Hang on! Who said anything about steady girlfriends?'

'Don't go all coy on me, Charlie Paddon. You've been on – how many dates is it? Five? Six?'

'Two. We've had one meal together and I met her with a group of her friends.'

'Didn't you take her to see that soppy film?'

'All right. Three dates. Jackie's just a friend. And it wasn't soppy. There were explosions.'

'Handy to have a friend on the BA ground crew. Means you can just happen to bump into her every time you're on duty at Heathrow. So that's three dates and how many bumps?'

'Give it a rest, Alex.'

'She's got a lovely arse.'

'I hadn't noticed.'

'I'll bet you...' She broke off as Charlie grabbed her arm.

'There!' he said, pointing towards the hotel entrance. A tall, black man in a crisp, grey suit had just stepped out from under the canopy. He checked the time – the sun glinted gold off his watch – and set off up the road.

'Paul Malamba,' he said. 'We can't both follow him, not with Saiki still in the building.'

'Toss you for it.'

'No, you stay here and keep an eye on the hotel. He's probably only nipping out for a smoke.'

Besides, he thought as he swung open the BMW's door, *it looks as if I'll have to get used to doing things on my own.*

5

June 25th

17:00

Cabinet Office, Whitehall

Henry Worthington stood at his office window, as the hot summer breeze carried in the chimes of Big Ben. It was a sound he never tired of, which was more than could be said of the smell. A problem with the drains, the surveyor had said. Whatever it was, the stench had been there a week and showed no sign of going away. Tomorrow they were bringing road-working equipment. Then it would be goodbye Big Ben and hello migraine.

He closed the window and loosened his tie. Time for a whisky.

Opening the bottom drawer of his desk, he brought out the bottle of twelve-year-old malt he'd been saving. Splitting the seal, he opened the bottle and sniffed. *The sweet scent of retirement*, he thought. All he needed now was some ice.

The phone rang. He put down the bottle and picked up the handset.

'Worthington.'

'Henry, this is Burfield. Since when did we give our foreign johnnies the run of the capital? D'you know what a position it puts my people in?'

Henry sighed. He thought he'd got away with it.

'Hello, Brian,' he said. 'I've been meaning to give you a call, but what with one thing and another ... you know how it is.'

'It's madness, that's what it is. First, I've got two of my best officers tailing the Limpopo president to the tobacconist. Then, his partner-in-crime goes off on another wild goose chase, forcing my team to split up. *Then* you leave a message with my office saying we should back off altogether and let Saiki and Malamba go wherever the hell they like. Is this a joke or what?'

'I don't actually recall using the words "go wherever the hell they like", Brian.'

'I'm paraphrasing. You know what I mean, Henry. We've got a job to do and you just made it six hundred per cent harder.'

Henry poured himself a generous measure.

Suddenly the ice didn't seem so essential. 'I think you're exaggerating, Brian,' he said. 'But I take your point. Look, it's all about balance. Yes, we need to protect visiting diplomats. But they mustn't feel crowded. Britain isn't a police state, however much you'd like it to be.'

'I'm not out to run the country, Henry. Just keep it tidy.'

'Of course. And all I want to do is make sure visitors to this country enjoy their stay. These visitors in particular. There are a lot of people very keen on securing the friendship of Messers Saiki and Malamba while they're here. I want them to feel completely at home.'

'So much at home they get blown up crossing Westminster Bridge?'

'You've been reading too many Jack McClintock editorials. Brian, of course I don't want anything to happen to them. I'm not asking you to stand down altogether. I just need you to be ... discreet.'

'I'm not backing down on this, Henry. If it's discreet you want, you'll get it. But we're not going away.'

'I wasn't asking you to. Low profile is all I ask. Was that everything?'

'For now.'

Typical SODs, Henry thought as he put the phone down. *Never give you an inch.*

He returned his attention to the whisky. He sipped it and let the richness melt into his tongue. He swallowed the rest, kept his eyes closed as it burned its way down his throat, then poured himself another. On his laptop, the screensaver caused images of Madeira to dissolve one into the next. In this heat, even Henry's favourite holiday destination failed to please.

Perhaps I should go somewhere different this year, he thought. *But where?*

There was a knock at the door.

'Come,' he said.

Eileen's cheekbones appeared. She'd just had her hair cut short. Given her natural angularity, the overall effect was like something conceived by the German expressionists.

'It's Nick Luard to see you, sir,' she said. She was using her haughty voice. 'He's aware he doesn't have an appointment.'

I'll bet he is, thought Henry.

'Show him in, Eileen,' he said. But Luard was already striding past her into the office. She scowled and slammed the door.

'Charming lady,' Luard said, throwing himself into a leather chair. 'Where do you find them?'

'Make yourself at home, Nick,' said Henry. 'What can I do for you?'

'Is that a single malt? You can pour me a glass, for a start.'

Henry obliged, wondering which was worse: SODs' flatfoot doggedness or MI6's superiority complex. Like every other spook he knew, Nick Luard assumed he could turn up any time, unannounced, and immediately have your undivided attention.

'I'll get straight to the point,' said Luard, taking a hefty swig of Henry's whisky. 'I need you to do some sniffing for me.'

'Do I get a licence to kill?' asked Henry.

'This is no joking matter, Henry. We're badly behind on this Republic of Limpopo business and we need a good lead. There's a lot at stake and I think you can help us fill in some blanks.'

'I'm flattered. Go on.'

'As you know, we've been investigating the alleged link between the Republic's former president Kissonga and certain business interests in the UK. The so-called "British connection" that allowed Kissonga to embezzle his own government out of millions of Rennits.'

'But how can I possibly help with that?'

'You can't, not directly. But Jack Mc-Clintock can.'

Henry's heart sank. He'd known that sooner or later his relationship with Jack would come and bite him on the arse.

'I'm not sure I'm with you,' he said, slowly.

'I think you are. Ever since his African trip, McClintock can't stop churning out copy about the Republic of Limpopo. And *The Times* can't stop publishing it. McClintock was right there when the bomb went off. He's the one who keeps dropping hints about British involvement. I want to know who he's talking to, and what they know.'

'What's that got to do with me?'

Luard sat back in his chair and rolled the whisky tumbler between his hands. 'Let's not play games, Henry. Jack McClintock's your brother-in-law, you don't have to work for MI6 to know that. Just ask him what's going on.'

'We're not that close.'

'You go round most weeks for Sunday lunch. Your sister, Mary, cooks you an extra casserole which you take home to put in your freezer. You're godfather to their two sons. Do I need to go on?'

'You're asking me to compromise my professional relationship with a member of the press...'

'A second-rate hack you use on a regular basis to leak rumours when it suits your department to do so. Is that the "professional relationship" you're talking about? Henry, I don't think you're listening to me. Once those mines are nationalised, the Republic of Limpopo government will be looking for a heavyweight industrial partner to help it process all those expensive rocks. There's every chance that partner could be the UK, but only if we can prove ourselves to have a clean track record. If there was ever any hanky-panky between Kissonga and a British citizen – or corporation – I need to know, and I need to know fast.'

'I thought that was what your people did: dig up information.'

Luard drained his whisky and slammed the tumbler down on the desk. 'Much as it pains me to admit this, sometimes we draw a blank. Henry – you just got drafted.'

Something about Luard's tone was making Henry uneasy. He didn't like being made to feel that way, especially in his own office. He stood, strolled to the window, stared over the Whitehall rooftops.

'It might not be that easy,' he said, at last.

Luard straightened the seams of his trousers. 'I'm sorry, Henry, but this really is the only way. My orders come from the very top, I'm afraid. Just talk to McClintock. See what you can find out. That way we can both keep Oliver Fleet off our backs.'

Henry turned, but Luard was already disappearing through the door.

Returning to his desk, Henry poured himself another whisky. To his surprise, his hand was trembling.

I've never seen Luard so edgy. This must be a bigger deal than I'd thought, if Oliver's leaning on him, too.

It came to something when the Cabinet's Security and Intelligence Coordinator – Henry's superior – sent the head of MI6 to put the screws on his own man.

Brian Burfield was right: where diamonds were concerned, people could get very excited.

Henry surveyed the clutter on his desk: the laptop, still running its screensaver; the mountain of documents he still had to read before he could retire to his Westminster apartment; the bottle of malt whisky. And the photograph of his two nephews, Tim and Jason. Jack's kids.

Just a quick chat, he told himself as he

dialled Jack's direct line at the paper. *It's practically old news now. Maybe he'll just come out with it and tell me.*

'Henry!' Jack was, as ever, ebullient. 'How's things, old man? Missed you last Sunday.'

'Yes, I'm sorry about that. Duty calls and all that.'

'Must have been a real bummer, that all-expenses-paid trip to Reykjavik. Care to tell your Uncle Jack all about it?'

'Nothing to tell, Jack. Deadly dull from beginning to end. I didn't even get to dip my feet in the volcanic spa.'

'A likely story. I'm sure they'll be writing up your escapades in the next Norse saga. Now, what can I do for you? I only ask because we've got a babysitter tonight. Your sister and me, we're painting the town red. Well, salmon-pink at least. You've got to ease back a bit at our age.'

'Well, I just wanted to pick your brains really.' *Here we go.* 'You know the Republic of Limpopo president's over here at the moment?'

'I'm writing a piece on him as we speak.'

'Oh. Right. Well, as a matter of fact, I'm writing something, too. A ... a report. On the previous administration. And I was wondering if you could clear something up for me.'

'Go on.' Suddenly Jack didn't sound so cheerful.

'It's this business about the Rennits. All that money vanishing out of the Limpopo economy. I just get the impression you know something about where it went.'

'You do?'

'Well, yes. In your articles you keep hinting that it ended up in the UK – or got laundered here at the very least. I just wondered where you're getting this information, Jack? What's your source?'

'I couldn't possibly say.'

Henry could almost hear the portcullis coming down. 'I wouldn't ask if it wasn't important, Jack. You know I'll be discreet. And it's not as if I haven't done you favours in the past.'

'This is different.'

'Jack, I'm not asking for much. There really could be a lot riding on this.'

'If there's that much riding on it, how do I know you'll be discreet?'

'I give you my word.'

'You're a bureaucrat, Henry. How much do you think that's worth?'

'More than the word of a journalist, that's for certain.'

'In your dreams.'

'Jack – I really must insist you cooperate. We're talking about national security issues here. You realise I would be quite within my rights to contact our legal department? Do you really want to make me do that?'

'I wasn't aware I was making you do anything, Henry.'

And up goes the drawbridge. Henry rubbed his hand across his forehead. 'Look – isn't there anything you can tell me, Jack? Between the two of us, I promise.'

'Us and a thousand spooks? Look, Henry, I'm not trying to be obtuse, but put yourself in my position for a minute. Let's suppose I was in possession of the information you need. Can't you see that, if I told you, and if that information then suddenly entered the public domain, the next day's headlines wouldn't be written *by* Jack McClintock. They'd be *about* Jack McClintock. About how an unknown intruder had inexplicably bludgeoned him and his loved ones to death and not even bothered to steal a single piece of jewellery from the family home.'

'Jesus.'

'A fellow I'm not ready to meet just yet.'

'You don't seriously think anyone would...'

'You know what, Henry? I'd just rather not

find out.'

Silence fell. Henry hated it when a conversation dried up; when you were on the phone it was even worse.

'All right, Jack,' he said at last. 'I'll leave you to finish up your story. Have a good evening. Give my love to Mary.'

'You coming over at the weekend?'

'Am I still welcome?'

Another brief silence. 'See you on Sunday.'

There was a click as Jack put down the phone.

Henry took another sip of whisky. Somehow it didn't taste the same. His nephews beamed at him out of the photograph. He'd taken the picture himself: a fishing trip, just him and the boys, last summer. The first occasion Jack and Mary had trusted him to whisk them off and keep them safe.

The picture was a close-up of the two lads at six and four. They were up to their knees in weed-ridden water and holding a colossal rainbow trout between them. Their grins went practically to the edge of the frame. They looked young and somehow invulnerable. Except, of course, they weren't.

He tapped the picture with his forefinger. Then he nudged the wireless mouse he used when his laptop was docked on the desk. Madeira vanished, revealing his email inbox.

Twelve new messages to read. And that mountain of paperwork wasn't getting any smaller. Another late night.

There was one thing he had to do before he started the late shift. Clicking the *New Message* button, he composed an email to Nick Luard.

Despite my best efforts, I regret I cannot supply you with the information you asked for. I am afraid MI6 will have to bite the bullet and gather the intelligence for itself. This should not prove too difficult as it is, after all, precisely what Her Majesty's Government expects it to do.

He hovered the cursor over the *Send* button without actually clicking it. Was sarcasm a good idea? If Luard really was under Oliver Fleet's cosh, it could backfire badly. With only six years to go until he retired, Henry Worthington was ever mindful of the vulnerability of his own position.

Sod it. The creep deserves everything he gets!

He clicked *Send.* If it cost him his OBE, so be it. It would be worth it to make Luard squirm.

As he took the first document off the top of the mountain, a question remained in

Henry's mind. Annoyingly, it was the very question Nick Luard had planted there:

Who was doing business with President Kissonga in the UK?

Whoever it was, were they really as dangerous as Jack seemed to think? If so, what would they do when they realised their rather lucrative gravy train was about to be derailed?

6

June 25th

18:34

Ye Grapes, Shepherd Market

The sign above the door said the pub was built in 1882. Paul Malamba wondered what his ancestors had been doing in that year. Probably fending off yet another attack from the Boers. The Zulus had come next. Life was like that in the Republic of Limpopo. In recent years it had been the enemy within: Kissonga.

Ancient history. It was time to focus on the future. On what happened next.

Stepping inside the pub, he might as well have been stepping back in time. Ye Grapes was a dark warren of low beams and shadowy snugs. The bar was packed with shirt-sleeved office workers letting their hair down, but deep in the recesses were characters straight out of Dickens: lean men with long noses and pale women wearing too much mascara. Stuffed animals glared down from the sepia walls. He inhaled, expecting to fill his lungs with smoke. But nobody smoked in pubs any more. Pity. All this fresh air ruined the atmosphere.

He found a space at the far end of the bar. A young blonde woman half his age gave him an appreciative smile. She was chattering into her mobile, but her eyes lingered on his as he squeezed past her and perched on a stool.

'A pint of London Porter,' he said, when the barman finally noticed him.

When the ale arrived, he drank half of it down in a single draught. Ah, there was nothing like warm British beer! The taste of it sent him time-travelling again. This time he went all the way back to his student days in York. Pub-crawls and midnight parties and the thick aroma of real ale. *Those were the days.*

He drained the glass and ordered another. He drank his second pint more slowly, savouring every mouthful. As he sipped, he gazed around the bar.

The pretty blonde was with a crowd of friends. Malamba guessed they all worked together. The men had loosened their ties and the women were all dressed in skimpy layers, showing their bare shoulders and arms. They were noisy and happy. He tried to remember the last time he'd seen a bunch of bright young things enjoying themselves like this in the Republic.

Enjoy what you take for granted, he thought. *You grumble about your relationships and your credit card bills, but you do not question the fresh water in your taps or the freedom you have to speak your minds.*

The blonde ended the call on her mobile. She pressed the phone against her lips, pouting against it as if she were on an advertising shoot. All the while she kept her eyes on Malamba. A young man whispered something in her ear and she draped herself over him, started giggling. Then her phone rang again, and she was chattering once more.

Malamba envied the girl her youth, and he envied the man the girl. Looking round, he saw countless more just like them – youngsters without a care in the world. The pub was alive with them, with their chatter. The chatter was so loud, he realised, because half of them were talking on their mobile phones.

He imagined lifting his hand and all the

phones falling silent. All of them, suddenly dead. He could do it, too. Not right away, of course, but given time.

You see, Mr Bond, most of these telephones have rechargeable lithium-ion batteries. Batteries with cathodes made from cobalt oxide. It just so happens that, as soon as my fiendish plans come to fruition, ninety per cent of the world's cobalt will be coming from the Republic of Limpopo mines. One word from me and a billion little RECHARGE bars will be forever dark.

He chuckled to himself as he downed the rest of his pint. He was no movie villain. But the power he wielded was real. And there were plenty who might not see him as exactly the hero.

Before he could flag down the barman, his own mobile rang. He flipped it open.

'Paul Malamba here,' he said.

'It's me,' said a man's voice. 'Where are you?'

'I am where we agreed,' said Malamba. 'In a pub just behind Mayfair. Called Ye Grapes.'

'Good. I'm on my way there now. Have you found a quiet spot?'

'We can talk privately, if that is what you mean.'

'That's exactly what I mean. I'll see you in

five minutes. Get the drinks in.'

Relaxed by the ale he'd already drunk, Paul Malamba set up another order and waited for his contact to arrive.

Hidden in a booth towards the back of the pub, Charlie peered over the top of his *Evening Standard*, trying to hear what Malamba was saying into his mobile. It was pointless: the bar was packed and the din was overwhelming. And he wasn't here to spy – just to provide covert protection. That didn't put a cork in his curiosity though.

Malamba finished the conversation and put his phone away. He was smiling as he did so. If he'd been a regular punter, Charlie would have guessed he'd just won on the horses or lined himself up a hot date.

But Charlie suspected any bets Malamba made were for rather higher stakes. Still, the latter was a distinct possibility. Shepherd Market was a regular haunt of wealthy visitors to London – businessmen and politicians alike. Its popularity had less to do with the narrow cobbled streets and quaint pubs serving real ale than the high-class hookers with their leather coats and gimlet eyes. Malamba might have been married with kids but he looked and acted like a smooth operator, with his tailored suits and gold jewellery; Charlie could just imagine him taking time out to lie down with one of the Mayfair girls.

Malamba took receipt of a third pint. At this rate he'd be fine with the lying down, not so good with the getting it up. Charlie smiled at the thought and sipped his own beer.

Malamba' s earlier walkabout had turned out to be a quick trip to the bank. He'd tolerated Charlie's presence but, unlike President Saiki, he seemed uncomfortable with his SODs escort.

'Do you have to shadow me all the time?' he'd asked, as he left the bank. After waiting outside, Charlie had fallen back into step with him.

'I'm sorry, Mr Malamba. I'm only doing my job.'

'Are you, officer?' Malamba had stopped and looked him in the eye. 'I think with you it is more than that.'

'I believe you need looking after, sir,' Charlie had said, looking right back. 'Don't you agree?'

Malamba had remained tight-lipped all the way back to the hotel.

Charlie had got back in the car only to

have Alex hand him a fax fresh off the BMW's built-in printer. The fax was from Brian Burfield.

'Bloody typical!' he said, scanning through it. 'Absolutely bloody ... Alex, have you read this?'

'Henry Worthington to a "T", isn't it?'

'*Whitehall has agreed with the Republic of Limpopo authorities that we shall adopt a hands-off approach with regard to any extra-curricular activity undertaken by President Saiki's companions.* You know what that means, don't you?'

'You're having a hernia?'

'It means Henry bloody Worthington's letting Paul Malamba wander about wherever he bloody well chooses, that's what it means. Let's hope assassins knock off at five-thirty, too.'

He balled up the fax and hurled it at the windscreen. It bounced off and landed in his lap.

'Brian's as unhappy about it as we are,' said Alex. 'He called just after he sent the fax.'

Charlie picked up the crumpled fax and stuffed it into the ashtray. When it didn't fit, he rammed it home with the heel of his hand. 'What did he say?'

'If you want to go plain-clothes this evening, he'll look the other way. If Malamba decides to go exploring again, Brian says you're free to tail him. Discreetly though. If he sees you, there'll be hell to pay.'

Charlie sighed. It made sense. Ever since SODs had risen from the ashes of the DPG, they'd been doing more and more close body work. 'Once upon a time it would have been SO1 playing gumshoe,' he said. 'Now it's just us.'

'It's better this way,' said Alex, 'and you know it. You remember the cock-up with that senator from Alabama?'

He did, only too well. It was back when they'd still been called the Diplomatic Protection Group. He and Alex had been parked outside the US Embassy in Grosvenor Square, waiting for their SO1 counterpart to turn up and chaperone the senator to wherever he was going. Only SO1, thinking the DPG had it covered, didn't show. It was early November and suddenly some kids had started letting off fireworks in a corner of the square. The Americans had panicked, the senator had been bundled into the back of Charlie's BMW and Charlie's foot had ended up flat to the floor. Embarrassing for everyone, not least the senator, who had to be driven back to his hotel so he could change his underwear.

Now SO1's surveillance responsibilities fell squarely under the SODs umbrella. Everything was simpler; everyone knew where they stood. The only downside was that surveillance work kept Charlie out of his beloved BMW. Under cover meant, not surprisingly, ditching the car with the bright red paint job and the high-visibility chequerboards along the side.

'Good job I keep my civvies in the boot,' he said, opening the car door. 'D'you think Dave Rodriguez can find me a spare hotel room to change in?'

'The rates they charge here,' said Alex, 'you'll be lucky to get a broom cupboard.'

Now, as he sipped his beer in Ye Grapes, Charlie thought about Alex still sitting in the BMW outside the hotel. While he was shadowing Malamba, she was watching out for Saiki. You never knew when an African president might start hankering after another box of cigars.

He wondered who Brian would partner him with after Alex had gone to Dubai. Karen Finnegan, maybe? More likely Big Johnno.

Paul Malamba stood up, turned towards

the door. A blonde girl at the bar looked him up and down, clearly liking what she saw. Charlie followed Malamba's gaze, expecting to see a slender woman with perfect skin slink her way through the crowd to begin her evening's trade. Instead, he saw a tall white man who appeared to have borrowed Richard Branson's hair for the evening. The man squeezed up to the bar and shook Malamba's hand. The two men smiled, exchanged a few words – foreheads almost touching so they could hear each other over the racket – then made their way over to a booth that had just been vacated.

As they crossed in front of Charlie, he ducked behind the newspaper. He didn't think Malamba would recognise him out of uniform, but you couldn't be too careful.

Charlie stole a cautious glance round the *Evening Standard*'s sports page. Malamba and his friend were already deep in conversation. Moments later a barmaid delivered more beer to their table. Malamba tipped her with a winning smile and she went away with flushed cheeks. He didn't have a hooker on his arm, but he was quite the lady's man.

Charlie wondered who the friend was. An old university chum? If only he could hear what they were saying.

'Long time since I've had a pint of ale,' said Paul Malamba's guest as he sipped his drink. 'I'm a lager man myself. Mind you – I'm buggered if I know why they call it "London Porter".'

'It was favoured by the porters at Smithfield Market,' said Malamba. 'Billingsgate, too, I believe. The original brew was a mix of three different ales...'

'All very fascinating.' Pettifer cut him off with a raised hand. 'But we're not here to talk about the beer.'

'I have been told you like to get to the point. Now I see it is true.'

'When you've been in the business as long as I have, you realise the "point", as you call it, is all there is. Small talk's for cocktail parties, Mr Malamba, and I don't see any daiquiris.'

'I understand. Where shall we start?'

'We'll start with you. Why don't you tell me exactly what you want?' Pettifer swept his hand back through his rock-star hair and smiled. For all his bullish approach, he looked suddenly charming.

'It is very simple. I want clever tools and clever men. I have something the rest of the world wants, but I need help to get it out into the marketplace.'

'Just so we're clear – you're not talking about the diamonds, are you?'

Malamba shrugged. 'I like diamonds. Who does not? Ours are small in size and plentiful in number. We are not about to produce the next Koh-i-Noor, but we keep a lot of drill bits turning. But there is already a well-established pipeline for processing the diamonds and, for the time being at least, I have no plans to disrupt that.'

'A pipeline that runs right through the middle of Johannesburg.'

'A problem that will be resolved, in time. I have ... plans. But, to answer your question, no – I have not asked you here to talk about diamonds.'

Pettifer swallowed back another mouthful and slammed his glass down on the table. 'Cobalt then,' he said. 'The next big thing. Why don't you tell me all about it?'

Malamba pressed his hands flat on the table and thought about what to say next. The pretty blonde at the bar had been abandoned by her companions. Now she was gazing at the back of Pettifer's head. For an older guy, he certainly had plenty of charisma.

But can he be trusted?

Malamba's intelligence said yes. And, given the stakes, he really had very little choice.

'It comes down to two issues,' he said, focusing his attention on his guest. 'The first is technology. As you know, we have been mining cobalt for some years, but not at significant volumes. Our smelting operation is antiquated and generates vast quantities of sulphur dioxide gas. Each year the environmental groups penalise us more and more. Electrolysis is beginning to take over but, frankly, the latest technology is hard to come by in southern Africa.'

'Electrolysis is hardly new.'

'No. And in a way, that is my point. As soon as the mines are under my control, I plan to introduce a next-generation extraction process: biochemical leaching, the same system that is used to extract gold. By using bacterial catalysts, I can make the entire cobalt industry faster and cleaner. And much more profitable. That is why I'm here in the UK: I need your expertise. Only last week I was reading an article in one of your science journals about improved ways of...'

Pettifer waved his hand. 'Let's not get bogged down with the nuts and bolts. What's the second issue?'

Malamba took a deep breath. 'Piet Bakker.'

Pettifer's silver eyebrows climbed towards his generous hairline. '*Now* this is getting interesting.'

Charlie wondered how long he could nurse his beer and read his paper without looking suspicious. Malamba and his friend were deep in conversation – getting deeper, judging by how close their heads were getting – and seemed oblivious to his presence. He still couldn't hear much, although he was sure he'd caught the word 'diamonds' a few times.

'Buy me a drink, mister?'

He looked up and saw a short blonde holding a tall glass.

'Looks like you've already got one,' he said, putting the newspaper down.

'Aw, but it won't last all night. I'm just planning ahead.'

She sat down on the bench opposite and sipped what looked like a white-wine spritzer. 'So what's in the news?'

'Plenty. Some politicians argued, some celebrities got divorced, some footballers scored goals.'

'You're funny.'

'I'm also...'

'My name's Tara.'

'Tara. Let's just say I'm not really looking for company this evening.'

The smile turned into a pout. 'I'll sit here and be very quiet.'

'I'm sure you will but I, er, I have a girl-friend.'

The smile came back. 'Really? What's her name?'

Charlie put down the paper. Why had he let himself get dragged into this? 'Well, she's not so much my girlfriend, more sort of...'

'What's her name?'

'Jackie.'

'What's she like?'

He pictured her at Heathrow in her BA uniform and said the first thing that came into his head. 'She's got a lovely arse.'

'Sounds like a marriage made in heaven. So, are you doing anything later?'

He'd hoped she'd just go away of her own accord. He really didn't want to cause a scene. 'Look, Tara – let's do a deal.' He took his badge out, leant forward and lay it on the table. 'You run along, and I won't pull you up for soliciting, even though I'm tech-nically still on duty.'

He tensed, half-expecting her to throw the

drink in his face. But she didn't even blink.

'That's a shame,' she said. 'Because right now I'm off duty.' She drained her glass and stood up. 'See you on the streets, big fella.'

When she'd gone, Charlie glanced nervously over to Malamba's table, hoping their exchange hadn't attracted attention. But the two men were huddled even closer, talking more furtively. The crowd at the bar, in contrast, was getting rowdier. The place was really rocking tonight.

He tried to remember what time Jackie came off duty.

'You must remember,' said Malamba, over the music from the jukebox, 'that everything I tell you is in the strictest confidence. This is a very sensitive situation.'

Again, the dismissive wave of the hand. 'Bakker's in the dark?'

'Of course. Do you think we are stupid? Currently, all our mineral wealth passes through Bakker's hands, one way or another. Those old smelting works I told you about? They are owned and run by Bakker. The electrolysis plants? Bakker again. He is everywhere. Africa's natural resources have made him a very wealthy man. When we nationalise the mines, all that will change.

He will not be happy.'

'Especially since his own motherland's trying to squeeze him out as well. I'll bet the Republic of Limpopo's been a lot higher up his list of favourite places since Mandela gave him the thumbs down.'

'Africa is changing. Even South Africa. Slowly, it is true. But Piet Bakker will never change. Like the dinosaurs, his kind will soon be extinct.' He paused. 'The sooner that time comes, the better.'

'So you'd be happier if Piet Bakker was out of the picture?'

'Of course. Why would I feel otherwise?'

A strange look passed across Pettifer's face, too swift for Malamba to track. 'Well, have no fear, Mr Malamba. Your secret is safe with me. Not that you'll be keeping it secret much longer.'

'Soon the whole world will know what I am doing. But not before the appropriate arrangements have been made.'

'What about Bakker? As cats go, he's a very, very fat one. He won't be happy when you come along and start licking up his cream.'

'Bakker's days are numbered. That is one reason I have asked for your help, to remove any possibility that he might jeopardise what we are doing. My only fear is that our new president might decide to throw him a lifeline. Saiki is a good man, but sometimes he is such a ... such a *politician.*'

Pettifer tossed back his head and laughed. 'That he is. But what did you expect when you climbed into bed with him, my friend? That he'd just roll over and play puppies?'

Malamba hesitated, slightly disturbed by the notion of sharing a bed with Mani Saiki. The truth was, he hated having to rely on anyone. Including Pettifer. Unfortunately, in a game as complex as this, he needed partners.

'It is my hope,' he said, slowly, 'that President Saiki will do the right thing. If he does not ... if for some reason he decides that Piet Bakker deserves a slice of the pie ... well, things become more complicated.'

'We won't let that happen.' Pettifer finished his beer and checked his watch. 'I think our business is done for today, and I'm afraid I have another appointment. You've been very frank with me, Mr Malamba. In return I shall apply both mind and resources to dealing with the issues we've discussed. Already I feel a plan developing. We'll meet again in a day or two. Does that fit with your schedule?'

'My schedule is flexible.

'Good. I'll be in touch. Now, if you'll excuse me, I'm running late.'

'A businessman's work is never done?'

Pettifer winked. 'Not exactly work, old man. I couldn't visit Shepherd Market without sampling a little of the local produce, if you know what I mean.'

After a brisk handshake, he was off. His crest of silver hair soared over the heads of the people at the bar like an exotic seabird.

Malamba remained at the table for a few more minutes, enjoying the noise from the bar and the smell of bodies and beer. Should he have another pint? Probably not. Three was plenty, and he had an early start tomorrow at the Republic of Limpopo Embassy. And that pretty blonde girl had gone. Never mind. This was no time to get distracted by the opposite sex. And he was, after all, a married man.

Feeling empowered – perhaps by his meeting with Pettifer, maybe just by the beer – Paul Malamba rose and made his way out into the narrow street. There were people everywhere – young, happy people, enjoying the warm evening breeze. He wondered how long it would be before he saw such scenes in his home country.

If his plans came to fruition, maybe that day would come sooner than expected. He wondered what Mani Saiki would say if he knew this meeting had taken place. Saiki liked everything above board – in some respects he was as much a stickler for red tape as Kissonga had been. If he knew what his Minister for Minerals was getting up to after hours, he might disapprove.

But what the President did not know could not hurt him.

Probably.

7

June 26th

07:49

SODs HQ, New Scotland Yard

Henry watched Burfield slurp tea from the chipped blue and white mug. The mug was belching steam like a cooling tower. It was a wonder it didn't take the roof of his mouth off.

'There's more in the pot,' said Burfield. 'I make it strong, mind.'

'No, thank you, I'm fine with my coffee.' Henry flipped the lid off the skinny latte he'd picked up on his way over. Dino's, the little pastry shop that also made fantastic coffee, was more or less en route from his flat near Westminster Cathedral. Compared to Burfield's brew, it looked and smelled like ambrosia.

'I thought I'd drop in,' said Henry. He tried in vain to make himself comfortable on the police-issue chair. It wasn't easy when only three of the legs wanted to touch the floor. 'I gather all was quiet on the Limpopo front last night?'

'Fortunately for us, yes. We're just lucky nobody tried anything on.'

'I thought we'd already laid this one to rest, Brian. And I have to say, I'm less than happy that one of your officers decided to tail Paul Malamba last night. What if he'd been rumbled? This visit is sensitive enough, without kicking off a diplomatic incident.'

Burfield scowled into his mug. Through the glass partition behind him, Henry could see glowing monitors and moving uniforms. He wondered how many cauldrons of tea it took to keep this lot functioning through the night shift.

'Then be grateful he wasn't "rumbled", Henry,' he said, at last. 'Look – I'm just doing the job I'm paid to do. And so are my officers. You say nothing happened last night. As far as I'm concerned, something did. One of your precious African ambassadors had himself a night on the town. Charlie Paddon felt he had no choice but to tag along. You should be grateful he's so committed.'

'I'd hardly call a few pints in a Mayfair

pub a night on the town.'

'Not the point, Henry, and you know it.'

Henry sighed. He might have known Burfield wouldn't let it lie. The man was Yorkshire Terrier crossed with Rottweiler. 'Brian, I didn't come here for an argument.'

'Well, you've got one. Don't these people realise they have enemies? Do they think it's all a game?'

'They are our guests, and this is a free country...'

'They're not free. Not to put themselves at risk. Not to put our reputation on the line.' He poured the rest of the tea down his throat. Henry waited for the steam to come out of his ears.

Retaining his composure with difficulty, Henry went on. 'But this is how they want to play it. We have to respect their wishes, Brian. It's called diplomacy. You should look it up in the dictionary some time.'

'Oh, do me a favour, Henry.'

'I do you a lot of favours, Brian. It's just that most of them you never find out about.'

'Meaning what?'

'Meaning I'm on your side. Look – what you see as Whitehall letting things slip is just another example of open government. Times are changing, Brian. Transparency is here to stay.'

'The day Whitehall's transparent is the day I put on tits and a tutu. I still say you're opening up gaps in our security big enough to drive a truck through.'

'You're blowing this out of all proportion.'

'A fleet of trucks. Those big ones they have on the *autobahns*. Double-decker trucks with sixteen wheels and trailers on the back...'

'I think we're done here.' Henry clipped the lid back on his latte.

Burfield leaned across his desk. Henry almost expected him to grab his wrist. 'Anything you want to share with me, Henry? Anything that might explain why you're so keen to keep these particular African ministers sweet? Anything you want to get off your chest? All in the spirit of transparency, of course.'

'Have you finished?'

'I could go on all day.'

'I'm sure you could, Brian. I'm sure you could.'

Henry made straight for The Mall, always good therapy when he was angry. It was so indomitably straight – walking it always calmed his temper.

Early as it was, the sun was already hot.

Overhead, the sky was brilliant blue, but lower down, behind Buckingham Palace, it was beginning to turn a sickly yellow. Storm clouds were swelling in the west.

As he walked, Henry alternately sipped his latte and cursed the SODs Chief Superintendent. How dare Burfield get him so riled? And how dare Charlie Paddon act contrary to his instructions and follow Malamba into a pub? Wars had started over less.

Gradually, The Mall worked its magic and the curses fell by the wayside. Soon it was just Henry and the coffee and the sun.

Until he noticed the man shadowing him.

The man was tall and lanky, with a scraggly beard. Henry was a fast walker but he was easily keeping pace. Henry stepped up a gear; the bearded man followed suit, puffing a little.

Coincidence. You're just jumpy because you've spent the morning with SODs. He's just in a hurry to get to work, like you.

The man was right behind him now. Henry was beginning to feel afraid. Foolish, too. He wasn't sure which was worse. Should he stop and confront the fellow? Or just keep walking?

Before he could make up his mind, the

man sneezed. *I recognise that sneeze*, thought Henry.

'Jack?'

'For God's sake, you old fruit – will you slow down?'

Henry dropped his pace; and his brother-in-law fell into step beside him. For a second the face didn't match the voice. Then he realised what had caused the confusion.

'Jack,' he said. 'When the hell did you grow that?'

His brother-in-law rubbed his chin. 'Gave it a try in Africa, liked it enough to keep it when I got back. I think it's very Hemingway. Mary says it's more Mr Twit.'

'Who's Mr Twit?'

'Mr Twit? Roald Dahl? It's the boys' favourite book. Haven't they made you read it to them yet?'

'Look, Jack,' said Henry, 'was there anything in particular you wanted? It's just that I've got a busy day ahead and...'

'Five minutes, Henry – that's all I need. I thought maybe a little walk?'

Henry stopped beside a litter bin and tossed his cup into it. He looked mournfully along The Mall, which had successfully wiped his mind clean of Brian Burfield, only to replace him with Jack McClintock.

'Five minutes. No more.'

They diverted to St James's Park. 'You're biting your nails again,' said Henry, as they crossed the grass towards the bandstand. 'I thought you'd given up that particular bad habit.'

'I had. I took it up again.'

'Is something wrong?'

'Oh no, nothing's wrong. Not unless you call having a libel suit filed against you and losing your job and ending up in the gutter wearing borrowed shoes and eating out of last week's fish and chip wrappers "wrong".'

Henry grabbed his shoulder. 'What? What are you talking about? You lost your job?'

Jack looked sheepish. 'Well, no. Not yet. But it's a distinct possibility.'

'Jack, just tell me what's going on.'

They found a bench and sat down. All around them people were on their way to work. Beyond the green of the park, London rose in blue haze. The sounds of the city seemed to come from very far away.

Henry realised it wasn't just the beard that was different about Jack – it was his whole demeanour. He looked like a man who hadn't slept in thirty-six hours.

Jack nibbled at his thumbnail. 'It's this Limpopo thing. All those articles I wrote. I swear, Henry, I've done nothing wrong. It was damn good journalism, all of it – no, don't look at me like that. It's just...'

'What?'

'Piet Bakker's says he's going to sue *The Times*. He says he's got us on four counts of libel and bloody Wilcox told me if Bakker bites, the best he can do is help pay for the face graft. It comes to something when your own editor won't back you up in a court of law.'

'Does Bakker have grounds? Be honest with me, Jack. Never mind all this "damn good journalism" nonsense.'

Jack buried all his fingers in his beard and scratched vigorously. 'Might as well get used to wearing this. They don't let you have sharp objects in prison.' He sneezed. 'Still, at least the hay fever won't be so bad. No pollen in solitary confinement.'

'You're just being melodramatic.'

'And Hemingway wasn't?'

'Actually, I don't believe he was.'

Jack sighed. Then he groaned. 'All right, yes – if I'm honest, Bakker's probably got me by the short and curlies. I just can't believe he'd want to expose himself like this. I mean, we both know I wasn't a million miles from the truth. Why would he risk even worse write-ups than he's had already?'

Henry let him run his tongue. Sooner or later Jack would tell him what this was *really* about. When he heard Big Ben chime the quarter hour, he instinctively checked his watch. He really did have a lot to do this morning.

'I'm sorry,' said Jack. Henry looked up sharply. He couldn't remember the last time his sister's husband had apologised for anything. 'I don't want to make you late for work. But there's something I wanted to ask you.' *Here it comes.* 'Some of your people must be keeping tabs on Bakker, given everything else that's going on at the moment. Isn't there any way you could arrange for some, um, some *pressure* to be applied? Someone could have a quiet word, you know. Tell him a lawsuit might not be such a good idea.'

'Tell him to back off, you mean?'

'It's my job, Henry. My livelihood. What would I do? You know what a struggle it is to save for the boys' school fees. You wouldn't want your nephews to end up in some comprehensive in Tower Hamlets, would you?'

That was below the belt. 'You do know how back-scratching is supposed to work, don't you, Jack? And now I'm afraid I really must be going.'

'Is that a yes? Will you put in a word?'

'I'm sure you'll work this one out for yourself, Jack. You always do.'

Henry set off back towards The Mall before Jack could detain him further. The cheek of the man, especially after he'd been so stubborn over Henry's request for information.

'Don't underestimate Bakker,' Jack called. 'He'll stop at nothing.'

Then stop broadcasting his name to the world! Henry doubled his pace; the sooner he was out of earshot the better.

'Those SODs of yours had better be on the lookout. As long as Piet Bakker's alive, the President of the Republic of Limpopo isn't safe to walk the streets. Hell, he isn't safe in his own country, let alone ours.'

Henry's gentle stroll had ended up as a forced march. It did nothing for his temper. By the time he reached his office he was beyond furious and heading for apoplectic. How dare Jack twist the emotional screws on him? And what was he thinking, shouting across the park like that? If he was really worried about Bakker making a move, shouldn't he be keeping his head down?

If he's right, we should all be keeping our heads down.

'Eileen,' he barked as he swept past her desk and into his office, 'get me SODs on the line. Right now.'

Outside the window, the pneumatic drills started yammering.

8

June 26th

10:13

Republic of Limpopo Embassy, Coventry Street

Paul Malamba descended the central staircase of the embassy two steps at a time. Halfway down, he had to duck to avoid the head of a Thompson's gazelle. He grabbed the worn mahogany handrail to steady himself and stopped to catch his breath.

The walls of the narrow stairwell were cluttered with mementoes of Africa. It was a hideous mix: stuffed and mounted trophies, tribal masks, colonial watercolours of the plains, spears ... it was utterly inappropriate for a small African nation trying to assert itself in the twenty-first century.

President Saiki – inevitably – had not been afraid to share his views on the subject.

'It causes me the greatest offence,' he had

114

said on his arrival at the embassy that morning, 'that my own people, detached from their homeland, have decided to celebrate their heritage by turning an official government building into a tacky-toffee souvenir shop.'

Faces had dropped. A pep talk had followed, concluding with instructions that an interior designer be hired immediately.

As a result, the mood in the embassy was subdued. In contrast, the president had been all smiles when he had received his first visitor of the day – a theme park developer with grand plans to build something called Safariland, right in the middle of the Mokatse Plateau.

Malamba stared at the glassy-eyed gazelle. How could Saiki demand a modernist interior for his embassy in one breath, yet sign up for a herd of fibreglass elephants in the next? It made no sense. Or perhaps it summed the man up.

He hurried on down the stairs, past the head of a hunting dog, set in a permanent snarl. The interior design was the one area in which he agreed with his president: the stuffed animals had to go.

Reaching the second-floor landing, he slowed a little. It looked as if he was going to make a clean getaway. Then the door to the conference suite swung open and there stood Mani Saiki. Not for the first time, Malamba was struck by how *vital* he was. Even standing motionless in the doorway, with his arms folded behind his back and his round face serene, Saiki still seemed packed with energy.

'Aha – Paul!' Saiki exclaimed. 'Just the fellow I wished to see. Come with me. I have finished discussing rollercoasters. Now it is time to talk about your precious rocks.'

'Really?' Malamba made a show of looking at his watch. 'I thought we had covered everything last night.'

'Oh, there is always something more to discuss,' Saiki beamed. 'Indulge me, minister.'

'Of course, Mr President.'

Before the window of the conference room they drank sweet tea and looked over the rooftops into Leicester Square. Tonight was the London premiere of the latest American blockbuster – a disaster epic about a giant tsunami hitting New York City – and people were already gathering outside the cinema. The sky above the Odeon looked yellow and foreboding, as if Hollywood had made special arrangements with the weather gods to create just the right atmosphere.

Malamba remembered the storm clouds he had seen on his way to Limpopo International Airport, and shivered.

'It appears to me that you are a little distracted this morning, Paul,' said Saiki. 'Would you care to tell me why that is?'

Because in less than two hours a South African mining magnate called Piet Bakker will enter this building and sit down with you. You in turn will tell him that his business empire will not last the year. I think I have every right to be distracted.

'It is nothing. Just a little jet lag.'

'Really? This is a big day for the Republic of Limpopo. The day I discuss with your former employer our grand plan to bring the mines under government control. I would not blame you for being nervous.'

The only thing I am nervous about is you striking a last-minute deal with that crook.

'Nervous? Well, perhaps a little.'

Saiki's eyes narrowed. 'Nervous. Yes, indeed. Tell me something, Paul. Do you consider Bakker to be an honest man? Is he someone the Republic of Limpopo government might do business with in the future?'

Malamba thought carefully about this. Was it a loaded question? 'I would not do business with that man for all the diamonds in the Republic of Limpopo's mines,' he said, at last. 'He is cruel and ruthless and cannot be trusted to hold to any promise he makes. The sooner we are rid of him the better.'

Saiki rewarded him with his broadest smile. 'There, once again I find myself in awe at your forthrightness, Paul. An honest politician. Who would have thought such a thing?' He leaned forward in his chair. 'Yet, it is a curious opinion to hold, is it not? For a man such as you, I mean. If Bakker is the villain you believe him to be, why did you continue to work for him for so many years?'

This was a question Malamba had asked himself time and time again, usually in the middle of the night. Alice understood his reasons, when he explained them to her in the darkness. He was not convinced Mani Saiki would.

'While I was General Manager at Bakker Diamonds and Minerals,' he said, 'I agreed with almost nothing Piet Bakker did. But as long as I was in a position of authority – which I was – and as long as he trusted me – which he did – I was able to make a difference to the way his company did business. Not the big things, you understand, but the little things. Things like providing canteens for the staff, or introducing compensation for injury, or keeping working hours within international guidelines. In short, all the things Bakker cared nothing about, and which mattered most to his workforce.'

Down in Leicester Square, the police were beginning to erect crowd control barriers in front of the cinema. Above the canopy, a huge cut-out tidal wave cast its shadow over the onlookers.

'A very praiseworthy approach,' said Saiki. 'But I am thinking: given your close relationship with Bakker – however troubled it might have been – I wonder if it might not be appropriate for you to attend this meeting? Were you present, you could ensure everything goes as you desire.'

Why was Saiki dangling this carrot now? All week he had been determined to deal with Bakker alone. That suited Malamba perfectly – the less actual contact he had with Bakker the better.

'You know my views,' he said, at last. 'As you said earlier: this is a big day. This is an announcement not of procedure but of policy. As such, it must come from the mouth of the president alone. We both know it would not be appropriate for me to attend.'

Saiki's eyes narrowed. 'So you trust me to

say the right thing?'

I trust you as much as the Americans trusted you to win the election without their support. Which is about as far as I could throw a pregnant hippopotamus.

'Of course, Mr President. Why would I not?'

Saiki clapped him on the shoulder. 'Very well said. And I agree with you wholeheartedly. Of what use is it for me to hold the stick if I cannot wave it once in a while?'

You fool, thought Malamba, leaving the room. *You are flattered when you should be scared. You prefer to meet alone with the man they call the Ice Axe. When you kick him in the teeth, do not be surprised if he kicks you back.*

As he made his way down the stairs, he felt a twinge of guilt. Not out of concern for Saiki – he did not really believe Bakker would try anything here in the embassy, however grim the news for his business. No, curiously enough, the guilt he felt was about Bakker himself. For all its failings, Bakker Diamonds and Minerals had been very good to Paul Malamba and his immediate family. Without such a solid platform to spring from, he might never have made the leap into politics. Was this really the way to repay that debt?

To answer that question, all he had to do was close his eyes and listen. Listen for the sound that still haunted him in the middle of the night. The sound of eighteen boreholes filled with ANFO exploding underneath his brother and their two cousins. There had been nothing left to bury – their bodies blown apart, turned to dust.

It was his big brother he missed most, of course – although Steven had been so small everyone assumed Paul was the elder. Steven was the only one who could match Paul at chess. Their games lasted days and often ended in stalemate. When Paul was at university in England, they had played distance chess by post; in later years they had played over the internet. Their usernames were Black Knight and Black Rook – Steven, always the unpredictable one, had been the Knight, while steady, reliable Paul was the Rook.

Neither brother had expected the Knight to be removed from the board so suddenly, and in such a violent way.

Nine years now he had lived without Steven. In the corner of the bedroom in his Limpopo City apartment, Paul Malamba kept a chessboard set up with the very game they had had in progress on the day Steven died. Each morning, when he woke and saw the pieces laid out on the board, he thought of all the possible ways that game might have turned out.

Was that weird? Had he built himself a shrine? Alice thought so, although she claimed to understand. Malamba was not sure she did, because for him the chess-board was a shrine to the future as much as to the past, and was therefore a symbol of hope. Every time he looked at that frozen moment, he told himself that anything was possible, that the endgame had not yet played itself out. That was a legacy Steven would have appreciated.

The truth was, the time had finally come for Piet Bakker to tip over his king and declare defeat. And if Malamba felt some small measure of guilt at stabbing his old boss in the back, well, he could live with that. Explosions at the mine notwithstanding, there were a thousand reasons why the corrupt bastard deserved it.

He checked his Rolex again as he trotted down the hall. The security people – what did they call themselves, Sods? – would be watching the front entrance, which was exactly why he was heading for the rear. They impressed him, these police officers with their body armour and their red cars. They were ... dutiful. None more so than the two he had seen most of: Paddon and Chappell. So here was something else to feel guilty about: giving them the slip like this, especially after his solo outing the previous night.

Duty, he thought as he plunged through the rear exit and out into the narrow alley leading to Shaftesbury Avenue. *That is what it comes down to.* Duty to the job, to your family. Above all, to your country.

Coming outside from the embassy's air-conditioned interior was like entering a sauna. *Or returning to Africa*, he thought as he pulled from his pocket the map he'd printed off the internet. Aligning it with the road, he got his bearings and set off towards Soho.

By the time he reached the end of Shaftesbury Avenue, the sky had turned black.

9

June 26th

11:25

Republic of Limpopo Embassy, Coventry Street

The clouds looked low enough to touch, black enough to chalk on. Warm wind poured down from Haymarket and whipped across the embassy's granite facade. It was as much as Charlie could do to stand upright. Beside him, Alex was leaning practically sideways in an effort not to get blown away.

'You said the forecast was "fair"!' she shouted.

'Never trust a weatherman,' he replied. 'Just our luck, too, when we're on red alert.'

'Let's hope it's a false alarm.'

Charlie doubted it was. Not judging by the look on Brian Burfield's face, when he'd called Charlie into his office first thing that morning.

'That journalist's put the cat among the pigeons,' Brian said, scowling.

'What journalist?' said Charlie. 'Come to that, what pigeons?'

'Jack McClintock. He's got Henry Worthington in a panic. Reckons Piet Bakker's got it in for President Saiki. Given what we know, that wouldn't be a surprise. Bakker might even be behind the recent assassination attempt. And, given that Bakker's actually meeting the president this morning, I don't need to tell you that puts us on special alert.'

'I guess this puts paid to Saiki's shopping trips,' said Charlie. 'He won't be happy about that.'

'I don't give a shit, Charlie. Let the man use Amazon like everybody else. Right now all I care about is getting him through this morning's meeting and back to Africa in one piece.'

Which was why Charlie and Alex had arrived at the Republic of Limpopo Embassy an hour ahead of schedule. They'd spent the extra time familiarising themselves with the layout of the building and acquainting themselves with the staff. In Charlie's experience, knowing first names could make all the difference in a crisis situation.

Toby, the overweight doorman, had taken

them under his ample wing.

'This place – it's my little African jewel,' he said as he gave them a tour of the ground floor. 'What you might call a "home from home". Only the new boss, between you and me, he says it's a little bit *too* much like home.'

'Let me guess,' said Alex, studying a Zulu shield someone had mounted on the wall over the downstairs cloakroom. 'President Saiki isn't one for souvenirs?'

'You could say that, ma'am.'

'We'd better watch for all this stuff turning up on eBay then,' said Charlie, winking.

Toby looked affronted. 'Officer! You think I'd dream of such a thing?' He stood, hands plunged deep into one of the rolls of fat at his waist. Then his enormous face broke into a broad grin. 'Me, I'm a car-boot man.'

Toby's laughter boomed down the corridors. He motioned to the handgun at Charlie's waist.

'You think you're going to need those?' he said.

'I hope not,' said Alex.

'Standard procedure, Toby,' said Charlie. He decided not to tell him about the MP5 submachine gun he'd be toting once he was standing guard outside.

Toby took them everywhere. He showed them the kitchens, the library, the security suite, the communications room ... he would have made a great estate agent.

'You're like a proud parent, Toby,' said Alex, when he took them out on the roof.

'It's my country, ma'am. I'm in this building, I'm home. You come through my door, officers, you're crossing the Republic of Limpopo border.' He held up a gold crucifix. 'Look at this.'

'It's beautiful,' said Alex.

'I won it off my brother. I beat him at poker. We had ourselves a three-month league and I just won that sucker.'

'Does your brother work here, too?'

'No, he's back home, in the Republic. But we play online and it's like we were never apart. And the best thing is, he gives this here crucifix to his boss Mr Malamba and Mr Malamba, he brings it right on over and gives it to me. Don't you think that's sweet?'

'Very,' said Alex, raising her eyebrows at Charlie.

'That Mr Malamba – he's one of the good guys.'

Bakker was due to arrive at eleven-thirty, so at five past Charlie and Alex took up their positions at the top of the front steps. They stood ten feet apart, either side of the double-door entrance; the granite columns and ornately sculpted lintel made this entrance a little more imposing than that of the cigar shop. And this time Charlie was cradling an automatic weapon.

Over the next twenty minutes, the wind blew in dark skies and the sharp scent of ozone. Thunder grumbled in the distance. Charlie tried to ignore it and concentrated instead on the crowds. Despite the storm, it was still summer in the city and the streets were packed with tourists. Why couldn't they have chosen a more discreet location for their embassy?

'At least it's early,' said Alex. She pointed down the road towards Leicester Square, where people were already gathering at the police barriers in anticipation of the big film premiere. Kurt Yeager, Hollywood's hottest new action hero, was due to lead the cast up the red carpet and there were plenty of fans getting ready to receive his signature in their autograph books or – just as likely – on parts of their anatomy. 'This evening you won't be able to move for the rich and famous. And the people who like to gawp at them, of course.'

'I know. I don't envy the Met boys that job. People think the police are killjoys at these red carpet events, but if someone gets killed, who carries the can?'

'The movie looks like fun, though. I always like to see New York getting trashed. And Kurt's a bit of a hunk. You taking Jackie to see it?'

The wind gusted, stronger than ever, snatching the reply from Charlie's mouth. A huddle of Japanese tourists bustled past, shouting at the tops of their voices, cameras held high. Close behind them were three tall women with deep tans and backpacks. They looked as if they'd walked all the way from the outback and were about to set out on the return journey. Two of them stopped to pose beside a red postbox while the third took their picture with her mobile phone. A sheaf of newspapers flew past them like a flock of seagulls.

'One thing's for sure,' said Alex, during a brief lull. 'I won't miss this weather.'

'You think they don't have storms in Dubai?'

'Oh ... well, I don't really know. But it can't be as bad as this.'

'You'll get sandstorms. It'll be like *Lawrence of Arabia*.'

'Or Lawrie of Arabia!' She laughed, just as the wind brought out its sledgehammer again.

Charlie was just considering taking shelter behind one of the stone columns when Piet Bakker's limousine came round the corner.

The sky lit up. Out of the corner of his eye, Charlie saw lightning connect the clouds briefly to some distant building. The lightning reflected off the roof of the limousine, a sharp white snap. The long, black car eased through the traffic and tucked into the kerb, blocking the path of a group of Hari Krishnas who were making their way towards Piccadilly Circus.

Charlie clicked his fingers towards the chauffeur. Alex obediently descended the steps to cover the front of the car, leaving Charlie to check out the back. When he reached the limo, he peered in through the rear window. In the middle of the back seat was a heavy-set man with dark glasses and a large briefcase. Piet Bakker.

As Charlie pulled open the door, the rain started coming down.

This was no summer shower – it was an instant deluge. It was as if all the humidity they'd suffered over the previous few weeks had gathered itself up and dumped itself on the city in a single cataclysmic downpour. Within seconds, they were soaked to the skin.

No matter. Bakker was getting out of the car. He was so big it was like a geological event. The chauffeur was getting out, too; in his right hand was a black, cylindrical object – Charlie's first thought was *truncheon*. The chauffeur extended his arm and the cylinder unfurled into an umbrella. He trotted round the car and held it over Bakker's head as he emerged.

Bakker's face turned towards Charlie's. It had the complexion of a concrete slab. The shades hid his eyes; Charlie felt as if the man were looking straight through him.

'Good morning, Mr Bakker,' he shouted. Thunder crashed above and the sound of rain was like static on the car's roof. Charlie's shirt clung like wet plaster. 'Follow me, please.'

In the street, people were rushing into doorways, under canopies. One couple wrestled open their umbrella, only to have it snatched inside out by the wind. The three backpackers – drenched and giggling – made straight for the embassy, but Charlie waved them back. Seeing his gun, they retreated with straight faces.

The chauffeur struggled to keep the umbrella in position, but Bakker seemed impervious to the rain. Nor did he appear to be in any hurry to make his appointment. He straightened his jacket and turned his head up towards the sky. The rain spattered on his tinted lenses. Only then did he begin a leisurely stroll up the steps. Charlie stayed close, frisking the man with his eyes. He didn't think he was wearing a shoulder holster, but Bakker's chest was so packed with muscle that it was hard to tell. Nothing obvious bulging in his pockets. Could he have a weapon strapped to his leg? And what about the chauffeur? Was the umbrella the only thing he was carrying?

Lightning flashed again as the embassy doors crashed open. Mani Saiki emerged, arms thrown wide in welcome, as heedless of the rain as his visitor. Wrong-footed, Alex turned from the limousine and raced up the steps towards the president. Behind her, the Hari Krishnas had reached Bakker's car and were streaming round it. The sharp sound of their bells pierced the rumble of the storm.

Alex overtook Charlie and the slow-moving Bakker. Just as she reached the president, Bakker tripped and fell.

Instinctively, Charlie reached out to catch

him. He might as well have tried to catch the Incredible Hulk. Bakker hit the steps hard and rolled into Charlie, nearly knocking him over. The chauffeur stumbled and dropped the umbrella; the wind snatched it up and tumbled it away down the street.

Somewhere a woman screamed, 'Get down!'

Charlie realised it was Alex.

Looking up the steps, he saw she'd drawn her Glock 17. The rain had plastered her hair to her head, her shirt-sleeves to her arms. She was raising her right hand – the one holding the gun – to point down the street. Her left hand was moving into place to support her forearm. Her legs were bent; she looked perfectly poised. Behind her, President Saiki flailed for balance. Charlie realised Alex had actually shoved the little man out of the way.

Charlie twisted in the direction Alex was aiming, as two blasts from a car horn punctured the air. The rain threw a gauze over everything. A black Audi, with its front passenger window down, hurtled around a stationary taxi. Sticking out of the window was the barrel of an automatic rifle. The instant Charlie locked his gaze on it, there was a starburst of light from the muzzle; a fraction of a second later came the crack of the gunshot.

From behind him came a scream. Charlie whipped round. Alex's gun was falling from her hand; she was falling too, sideways on to the steps. When she hit the stone slab she groaned.

Charlie's autopilot kicked in. His arms locked themselves round Bakker's shoulders. Something delivered him the strength to heave this Titan down the steps to his limousine, now mercifully clear of orange-robed Buddhists.

Two more gunshots cut through the howl of the wind. Stone chips flew from the corner of one of the embassy pillars. Another shot took all the glass out of one of the doors. Saiki ducked, then stumbled to his left, feet crunching through the broken glass. Charlie waited for him to fall – clutching his chest perhaps – but he didn't. He continued his random dance steps for another second or two, then froze, eyes and mouth wide.

Charlie had managed to wrestle Bakker up against the door of the limo. His body was working entirely of its own accord. Conscious thought seemed to play no part at all. 'Don't move!' his mouth yelled. 'Keep your head down.'

Bakker didn't argue. Hoisting the MP5 over the limousine's boot, Charlie's eyes stared out through the rain. All he could see was London clichés: red buses and black cabs and tourists. *Where the hell is the Audi?*

At the top of the steps, Mani Saiki was still standing alone and totally exposed in the doorway of the embassy.

Alex lay at his feet.

Thunder boomed directly overhead and Charlie came back into his body with a snap.

'Get inside!' he shouted at Saiki. The president didn't move. Inside the lobby, through the hole in the door, Charlie saw movement. 'Toby, if that's you, get him inside now!'

It was, indeed, the giant doorman. At the sound of his name, he kicked the shattered door off its hinges, rushed out and hustled Saiki back inside.

Once more lightning ripped open the sky; close behind the flash came a massive crash. Charlie heard a woman's voice shouting, 'There! There!'

It was one of the backpackers he'd waved off the steps. She was pointing up the road with her mobile phone. Charlie looked just in time to see the Audi screeching round the corner and disappearing down Haymarket. All the windows were up; the gun was nowhere to be seen. Worst of all, he hadn't caught the registration plate.

Grabbing his radio, he shouted into it: 'This is seven-twelve, SODs. We have a code red, repeat, code red emergency. Shots fired on Coventry Street. Officer down, repeat, officer down. Request immediate medical and tactical support. Repeat, this is a SODs code red emergency. All units respond immediately.'

Protocol dealt with, what mattered next was Alex. 'Stay there,' he barked at Bakker, and scrambled up the steps to where she lay.

Her body was twisted awkwardly, lying half-on and half-off the topmost step. Her face was white. Her hair lay straggled like something washed up on the shore. She stared up at him, panting rapidly, green eyes wide.

'Shot me, Charlie,' she croaked. 'Fuck.'

'Don't talk,' he said. 'Don't do anything. You'll be fine. The paramedics are on their way.'

'Fucking doctors. They said … twenty-one hour labour was … normal … what do they fucking know about…'

Her eyes closed and her voice trailed away.

136

Charlie resisted the urge to shake her, just held her shoulders instead. 'Alex!' he shouted. He hunched over her to stop the rain lashing her face. 'Alex – keep your eyes open. Look at me!'

He touched her cheek. It was ice-cold. Where the hell was the ambulance? He looked down her body, tried to see where the bullet had gone in. There was no sign of a wound. Maybe she'd been lucky. Maybe she hadn't been hit at all.

Then he saw the blood. It was pooling beneath her, spreading in a watery slick across the step. He watched, horrified, as the blood reached the edge of the stone flag on which she lay and started dripping down on to the next step.

Pressure. Got to apply pressure to the wound.

There, near her waist, in the narrow gap between her belt and the bottom of her bulletproof vest: a knot of white fabric, rapidly turning red. Charlie ripped open the vest, pressed his hand hard against the bloodstain. Beneath him, Alex moaned, but she didn't open her eyes.

'Hang in there, Alex,' he said. 'Help's on its way.'

Far away, he heard the wail of a siren.

10

June 26th

11:39

Cabinet Office, Whitehall

'Is the president all right?' asked Henry, gripping the handset so tight it creaked. 'Was anybody else injured?'

'The president's fine,' said Burfield. 'Alex Chappell's the only casualty – don't you think that's enough?'

There was an iron quality to Burfield's voice – Henry couldn't remember hearing it before. 'Yes, of course, Brian. That isn't what I meant. How is Sergeant Chappell? Is it serious?'

'She's on her way to UCH. We'll know more later.'

'Tell me what happened, Brian. Tell me everything.'

There was a pause at the other end of the line. Was he taking a swig of his revolting tea? Or just marshalling his thoughts? Henry waited. Outside, the sky turned from black to pewter as the storm passed over.

'All we know for certain, is someone took pot-shots at the embassy from a passing car,' Brian said at last, his voice sounding normal again. 'Automatic rifle. We'll know more when we've analysed the bullets.'

'How many shots were fired?'

'Four. The first one hit Alex. The other three just redecorated the front of the embassy.'

Henry closed his eyes. Talk about a near miss. If one of the bullets had hit Saiki... 'Thank God,' he breathed.

'What? Thank God Alex was hit? Girl's a bloody hero, Henry.'

'Of course ... that isn't what I meant. I'm just glad Saiki's safe. This was a close one, Brian. Although I have to say, as assassination attempts go, this was hardly a professional job.'

'Assuming it was Saiki they were after.'

'Well, of course it was Saiki. What else do you know? What about the car?'

'Nobody saw the number plate but we're hoping it's been caught on camera. We're on to that right now. It was a black Audi saloon, no distinguishing features. Pick any major corporation you'll find a dozen like it in the executive car park every morning. We'll probably find it burnt out on the Isle of Dogs before the day's over.'

There was another pause, and a long sigh. Henry gave him time – policemen got cranky when other policemen got injured. Hardly surprising, he supposed. As if to confirm this, Burfield said, 'I just got off the radio to Charlie. He's pretty shaken up by the whole thing. No more than you'd expect. He's fuzzy on what actually happened, but he reckons Piet Bakker tripped on the steps a second or two before the shots were fired. He thinks Bakker might have fallen deliberately, to give the gunman a clear line of fire.'

Henry was glad Burfield couldn't see him smiling. 'I hate to say, "I told you so," Brian,' he said. 'But what was I saying to you only half an hour ago? Jack McClintock told me there was going to be trouble today, and he was right.'

The iron returned to Burfield's voice. 'What you said, Henry, was that Bakker himself was the threat. Paddon's theory is all very well, but if Bakker really was out to get Saiki, why would he put himself in the firing line at all?'

'Because it's a perfect alibi!' said Henry, triumphantly. 'Who would suspect him of foul play when he might have ended up with a bullet in the brain?'

He leaned back in his chair and admired the plaster cornice.

The initial shock of the news was wearing off; his mind was turning its wheels again. Henry wondered if Burfield's was functioning as efficiently. Maybe it was time to let Whitehall to do the detective work and leave the flatfoots to pound the beat.

'It's a possibility,' said Burfield. 'Trust me, we're working on it. But there's something else – we've just done a head count at the embassy and it turns out somebody's missing.'

'Who? Not the president. Please don't tell me you've saved him from a bullet only to let him...'

'No, Henry, not the president. Mani Saiki is currently safe and sound in his private office drinking sweet tea and planning his next shopping expedition. No, the person who's missing is Paul Malamba.'

'*Malamba*?'

'Yes. And there's more. The doorman told us he saw Malamba leave the embassy by the rear exit earlier this morning. He didn't say anything at the time because he says it was Malamba's own business and none of his. We had to push him to tell us even that much – very loyal to his minister, that one. Malamba hasn't been seen since. Which is odd, given that we thought he was bound to attend the meeting with Bakker. It was supposed to be the big crunch moment after all. You'd have thought he'd want to be there, unless...'

'Unless he knew what was going to happen and decided to be somewhere else.'

'Exactly. One thing's for certain: Malamba knew when Bakker and Saiki were going to be on the steps together.'

Henry swallowed hard. This was getting more complicated by the minute. Maybe he was best leaving it to Scotland Yard after all. 'Then find Malamba,' he snapped. 'Do it fast and tell me the minute you've got him in custody. In the meantime, I'm going to call the Permanent Secretary and tell him this particular performance of *The Lion King* is well and truly over. I want President Saiki and his elusive Minister for Minerals bagged and tagged and on the first flight out of here to the Republic of Limpopo. They can fight over shiny stones on their own turf.'

Halfway through this tirade, Eileen poked

her head round the door. Unfazed by his temper, she held her forefinger up to the side of her head: shorthand for, 'You've got another call waiting.'

Henry waved her out angrily, concluded his conversation with Burfield and slammed down the phone. Clamping his hands behind his head, he marched to the window and stared at the receding storm. Already the sun was breaking through the clouds, as if nothing had happened. As the last of the thunder boomed in the distance, another sound kicked in much nearer to hand – right under the window in fact. The workmen with their fucking drills again.

He stretched and listened to his vertebrae pop. Walking to work kept him fit but he didn't like the way his back kept playing up. Maybe it was time to rejoin the archery club, get those muscles stretching again. First he had to put Africa to bed.

It was beginning to look as though Nick Luard was right. Maybe Paul Malamba really wasn't the wonder boy the Americans thought he was. Could this all be a plot to further Malamba's own political career? He was Saiki's natural successor, after all.

And, given his mining connections, Paul Malamba would have been well-placed to get his hands on enough high explosive to, say, blow up a bridge.

He's got his eye on the presidency. And he doesn't care who he's got to kill to get there.

The phone was flashing. He'd forgotten about the other call. He returned to his desk.

'Worthington,' he said, picking up the receiver.

'Ah, Henry,' said a voice that made him sit up straight in his chair. 'I was rather hoping you could fill me in on recent events at the Republic of Limpopo Embassy. From what I gather, it's all looking rather regrettable.'

'Permanent Secretary,' said Henry, adding just the right dose of honey to his words, 'I'm so glad you called. As a matter of fact, I was just on the other line trying to call you. I'm afraid the time may have come to reconsider our position regarding our African guests. You see, one or two interesting facts have just come to light...'

11

June 26th

12:02

Trumper, Curzon Street

Paul Malamba had spent the morning in one of the record shops he had located the previous night after his meeting in the pub. Nostalgia, he had decided, smelt of damp cardboard and vinyl. Speakers high on the poster-caked walls had blared non-stop eighties compilations – exactly the music Malamba and his friends had been listening to at York, all those years ago. The music had been so loud he was hardly aware of the storm outside. Searching through the boxes of records was a bit like mining: a lot of crap shot through with the occasional seam of gold.

The gold he found he bought: a post-Gabriel Genesis LP that had been missing from his collection for years, a handful of

Depeche Mode and The Stranglers, and Michael Jackson's 'Thriller'. An eclectic mix. He could not wait to get them back home where he could stack them up on his old turntable. Alice would groan and the children – well, they would just laugh at how ridiculous music had sounded in the old days.

Satisfied – and with his purchases safely wrapped in a black plastic bin bag – he had hurried through the rain to Mayfair to keep his midday appointment at Trumper. The storm was passing over; while he ran the rain stopped altogether.

It was Jimmy Fenchurch who had introduced him to the delights of Soho. Along with fellow students Baz Smith and Simon Garrett, Paul and Jimmy had made regular visits to the capital during their time at York University. Baz and Simon would lobby for fast food and all-night films, while Jimmy was continually seeking ways to introduce them to what he called 'culture'. In Jimmy's opinion, 'culture' included such diverse delights as opera, prostitutes, classic vinyl and grooming.

When Malamba confessed he had never used a cut-throat razor, Jimmy had thrown up his hands to the heavens.

'Then you haven't lived, old man!' he'd exclaimed. 'You're coming with me, right now.'

Thus had Paul Malamba found himself frogmarched through London to an elegant shop on Curzon Street. The shop window had been full of gentlemen's toiletries and the sign on the dark-wood panelling had informed him that the establishment had been in business since 1875.

'Behold Trumper,' Jimmy said, in a resonant undertone that was almost Biblical. 'One of the seven wonders of the modern world.'

'What are the other six?' asked Malamba.

Jimmy turned to him, flicked back his devilish fringe and said, 'Who cares?'

Thirty years on, stepping over the threshold of Trumper was exactly the same magical experience it had always been. Nothing had changed: the mahogany-panelled walls were the same; the smell of sandalwood was as sharp and evocative as ever. Even the staff looked the same, with their natty waistcoats and brisk smiles.

Malamba stood in the doorway, momentarily perplexed. How could a place be so old, and yet never change? He was suddenly aware of all London around him, of its tremendous age. The Romans had built here, and they had by no means been the first. Limpopo City was a mere toddler by comparison. For all its heritage – for all its claims to be the cradle of humanity – Africa was still the new kid on the block. Would it ever be considered civilised by its neighbours?

A white-haired barber greeted Malamba and checked his name on the register. 'Is this your first visit, sir?'

'I came once before,' said Malamba. 'A friend brought me, many years ago.'

'Ah yes, even in this day and age, word of mouth is still our favoured means of promotion. To you he is a friend – to us he is an ambassador.'

The barber ushered him into a private booth and closed the green velvet curtain. 'We pride ourselves on tradition, sir. Recently, however, we have started offering pedicures,' He bent close and whispered. 'If you ask me, sir, that's going a little too far. I mean to say, can you imagine Ian Fleming coming here in the old days and asking for a pedicure?'

'Ian Fleming came here?'

The barber tapped the side of his nose with his forefinger. 'I couldn't possibly say, sir.'

Malamba took the cape he was offered. Before putting it on, he looked round for somewhere to put his records. The barber, he realised, was eyeing the bin liner with distaste.

'Is there something sir would like us to dispose of?' he asked.

'What? Oh no, thank you. I will just rest these on the counter, if I may. Can we get on with the shave, please?'

'Of course, sir.'

The leather chair creaked luxuriously as it tipped Malamba backwards. The sense of both peace and vulnerability was exquisite. Quietly, in the next booth, a radio was playing Ravel's 'Bolero'. Malamba settled back and the barber wrapped hot towels around his face.

Malamba enjoyed the sensation while the old man prepared the tools of his trade. After a minute or so, the towels were taken away.

'With your permission, sir, I shall use our special balm. We find dark skin is so susceptible to razor bumps. We must do everything in our power to stop the hairs curling under and becoming a source of irritation.'

Malamba was beginning to find the barber a source of irritation. Why was that? Was it that you could never go back? Or was he simply annoyed by the man's sycophancy?

'Whatever you think best,' he said. 'But please, hurry up: I have a lunch appointment.'

The barber's lips thinned. 'Of course, sir.'

Out came the badger brush and on went the balm. As the barber lathered up his face, Malamba forced himself to relax again. It was hard. Although he had tried to put it to the back of his mind, he was still concerned about what Mani Saiki might say to Piet Bakker. That was what this visit to Trumper was really about – this and the trip to the record shop. It wasn't nostalgia at all. It was distraction.

In half an hour Saiki's meeting would be over, and the plans Paul Malamba had worked for so many years to construct would finally have been presented. The worst would be over. The hard work would be yet to come but, strangely, he thought then he might *really* be able to relax.

In the next booth, the music concluded. The station announcer wrapped up the section on Ravel, then an energetic man started talking about a half-price sale at a sofa warehouse. It was a while since Malamba had listened to British radio – he had no idea the classics had gone commercial.

The barber flicked the blade open on his cut-throat razor. It was a practised movement, like a magician's sleight-of-hand. Light from the wall-lamp glinted off the blade and Malamba felt the same brief thrill he had felt all those years ago.

The barber began his work.

The adverts on the radio finished abruptly. A woman announced that they were interrupting the programme for some breaking news. Without knowing why, Malamba tensed in the chair. Over the rasp of the razor, he heard the newsreader.

'Reports are coming in of an incident near Leicester Square. Shots were fired at the Republic of Limpopo Embassy in Coventry Street, resulting in the wounding of a police officer. There are no reports of further casualties. The shooting comes just weeks after a failed assassination attempt on the life of Mani Saiki, the Republic of Limpopo's new president. President Saiki, who is visiting the United Kingdom as part of his...'

Malamba did not wait to hear the rest. Throwing off the cape, he lunged forward out of the chair, quite forgetting he had a razor at his throat. Luckily, the barber's reflexes were as sharp as his blade, which he snatched out of the way.

'Sir!' said the barber, mildly. 'I really must ask you to...'

But Malamba was already pulling the curtain back and running for the door. Lather puffed from his face. The sound of the radio faded; the cries of the barber grew louder. Louder still – and getting louder with every step he took – was the thud of his heart in his chest.

Shots were fired...

An adjacent curtain twitched aside, revealing the round and curious face of another barber. A second face popped up from behind the counter. Where were they all coming from? Expecting to be challenged, Malamba yanked out his wallet and tossed a handful of bills at a man in an apron who had materialised near the door. He did not bother to check what denomination they were – nor even what currency. They seemed to satisfy the man however: having caught them deftly, he unlatched the door and touched his forefinger to his temple, allowing Malamba to fly headlong out into the street.

The pavement was wet from the rainstorm and he nearly skidded all the way out into the road. A refuse lorry growled past, its driver leaning on the horn as the big wing mirror came within ten centimetres of Malamba' s head.

Spotting a black cab at the end of the road, he grabbed a lamppost for balance and waved his arm. 'Taxi!' he yelled. 'Taxi!'

People were looking at him strangely. He carried on shouting, which just attracted more attention. Belatedly, he realised he was still covered in lather, which was now dripping from his chin. It did not matter. All that mattered was what he had heard on the radio.

Kissonga's people! It has got to be!

First the bridge, now this. It was too much of a coincidence. Could there be a cell of exiled supporters here in London? It was possible: unlike America, the UK had never openly condemned Kissonga's regime, had even supported it on the quiet, especially in the early days. Whatever channels had been open then would still be open today. Kissonga might even have orchestrated the attack himself from his Botswanan bolt-hole.

The taxi pulled up. The cabbie stared at him open-mouthed as he tugged open the door. Then he stopped.

They will know I sneaked away.

Malamba knew from a conversation he had overheard earlier between Charlie

Paddon and his partner that SODs had expected him to attend the meeting at the embassy this morning. He had not said anything to suggest otherwise. He had just bowed out at the last minute. By now they would have searched the entire embassy and discovered he was not there. Suspicious. He even had an idea Toby the doorman might have seen him leave via the rear exit. If they spoke to him...

He needed time to think.

'I am sorry,' he said to the cabbie, slamming the door shut again. 'I made a mistake. Please, go on.'

'Hope they only charged you half,' said the cabbie, nodding his head at the left side of Malamba's face.

Feeling sick, Paul Malamba began making his way on foot towards Piccadilly. He ignored the curious stares from passers-by. He was more concerned about the predicament he suddenly found himself in. In fact, he could not have made himself look more suspicious if he had tried. Never mind elaborate conspiracy theories about some hit-man hired by ex-President Kissonga, half a world and an entire continent away – what about the shifty minister who had left the embassy building barely an hour before he was due to take part in a high-level meeting, and who had not been seen for the rest of the morning?

In the distance he heard a squeal of tyres. A blue flashing light was weaving through the traffic. Seconds later, a car materialised beneath the light. The car was bright red, with a chequerboard of day-glo yellows and blues plastered down the side. He recognised it at once: it was SODs, diplomatic security, the very people whose job it was to make him feel safe.

Watching the car accelerate towards him, he felt anything but.

The red car skidded to a halt, tyres mashing against the kerb. The door flew open and the driver leaped out. He was tall, broad-shouldered and furious as hell. In his right hand he carried a small black handgun. It took several seconds before Malamba realised the man behind the angry expression was Chief Inspector Charlie Paddon.

As Paddon ran up to him, he realised something else. He had left his eighties vinyls behind in the damned barbers. He wondered if he would have time to go back.

The look on the Chief Inspector's face told him that was unlikely.

12

June 26th

19:21

University College Hospital

Slipping through the lift doors, Charlie found himself sandwiched between two pairs of nurses. The first pair looked as though they'd stepped off the front of *Vogue;* the others looked like Toby jugs. He nodded and smiled and wished he'd had time for a shower. His uniform was hardly fresh. But it had been a crazy afternoon, dealing with the aftermath of the shooting. And he was keen to see Alex on his way home.

All the nurses got out at the next floor, giving him a moment alone. He spent the time straightening the corners of the battered box of chocolates he'd picked up from the shop on the way in. If nothing else it stopped him replaying the scene outside the embassy for the thousandth time. He'd bought a copy of the *Evening Standard* too. The picture on the front page had caught his eye.

The lift doors opened and Charlie stepped out. Immediately, from the end of corridor, there came a series of loud bangs. His hand automatically snapped to his waist, before his mind caught up. At the end of the corridor, a large woman was manhandling a dinner trolley through double doors. Having taken out the first door, she was now ramming the trolley repeatedly into the second; the impacts sounded exactly like small arms fire.

'You all right, son?' said a voice. It was a wizened porter, on his way into the lift. He looked old enough to be on the geriatric ward.

Embarrassed, he stood and combed his hand back through his hair. 'I'm fine,' he said. 'The sound of the... I was just startled for a minute.' Behind him the lift doors closed. 'Oh, I'm sorry, did you want...?'

'It's all right – I'll get it next time,' said the porter, pressing the call button. 'Nerves are a terrible thing, you know. I wanted to join the police but they wouldn't let me on account of my nerves.'

'Really?'

'Oh yes. But you don't look the nervous type, son. Reckon you just had a bad day.'

The lift returned and he jumped inside. *Sprightly for an old codger.*

'Could you tell me where Room G17 is, please?' said Charlie.

'Down the corridor, second left, past the fish tank, left, right, third left and Bob's your uncle. Numbers on the doors. Watch out for matron. She's a Tartar.'

'Thanks.'

The doors closed, leaving Charlie to navigate the clean white corridors, reciting the porter's directions in his head as he went.

Matron turned out to be a pretty Irish girl who was more than keen to show Charlie to Alex's room.

'She's quite a lady, that one,' she said as Charlie went in.

'Yes,' he said, 'she is.'

A man with cropped sandy hair was standing beside the bed, with his back to the door. Charlie hesitated. If the doctor was examining her, maybe he should...

The man turned round. 'Hi, Charlie,' he said. 'We were just placing bets on when you'd turn up. It's before eight so it looks like I won, which means my wife owes me a quarter of a million pounds.'

'Lawrie,' said Charlie. 'I thought you were in Aberdeen.' He'd met Alex's husband several times before and wondered why he hadn't recognised him right away. Too intent on the patient, he supposed.

'I was,' said Lawrie. 'As soon as I heard about the shooting I jumped on a plane and came straight down here. Call me old-fashioned, but when you hear your wife's been shot it's kind of hard to focus on your work.'

'It's good to see you again.'

'Good to see you, too.'

'Uh, excuse me,' said Alex, from the bed. 'Gunshot casualty in need of chocolate here. I take it that's what's lurking in your hand, Charlie?'

'What? Oh, yes.' He handed over the box with a sheepish grin. 'Sorry, it's a bit mashed – it was all they had.'

'Build a girl up, why don't you?'

She was propped up in the bed with her shoulders resting on three large pillows. On the table beside her were two huge vases of flowers. From the carnations dangled a card bearing handwriting Charlie identified instantly as Brian Burfield's. The roses, he guessed, were from Lawrie.

As Alex took the chocolates she winced.

Instantly both men leaned towards her. 'Are you okay?' they said, in unison.

Alex stared at them, burst out laughing, but quickly stopped. Face contorted, she clamped her hand to her left side. 'Shit!' she said, under her breath. 'Got to stop doing that.'

'Here,' said Lawrie, reaching for the chocolates, 'I'll get those for you.'

'Hell you will,' she said, scooping them up. 'These are essential therapy. Doctor said so. *Shit*, that hurts.'

'What did they say?' said Charlie. 'I mean, how bad is it?' It was no fun seeing her in pain – although at least she was in one piece.

'Could be worse,' she replied, opening the box and prising out a caramel. 'Bullet went clean through and out the other side. Missed everything important – ribs, diaphragm, kidneys. Makes you wonder what's in there that's any use at all.'

'You seemed to be bleeding pretty badly on the steps.'

'Sorry if I got any on you.'

'Give me a chocolate, we'll call it quits.'

'Hey, is that the paper? Am I in it?'

Charlie took the *Evening Standard* from under his arm and tossed it on the bed. The

160

three of them looked at it in silence.

POLICEWOMAN BLOCKS BULLET

Beneath the headline was a large colour picture showing the front steps of the Republic of Limpopo Embassy. Lying at the top of the steps was Alex. Halfway up the steps, frozen in mid-run, was Charlie. The light was eerie – somehow grey and orange at the same time. Storm light, or maybe just bad printing. The picture was a little blurred, as if it had been taken by a shaking hand.

'Bloody hell,' said Lawrie. There was the tiniest tremor in his voice.

'You said it, baby,' said Alex. 'How did they get this, Charlie?'

'Citizen media. One of those backpackers used the camera on her mobile. The picture was on the Reuters website within an hour. It'll be pretty much everywhere by now. If it's any consolation, there's just as much coverage of the failure of Kurt Yeager to turn up to the London premiere of his own movie. Apparently Kurt's minders got a bit jumpy and put him on the first plane back to LA.'

Alex stared at the photo for a moment, then turned the newspaper over. 'I'll read it later,' she said, quietly. She beckoned Lawrie close and placed an orange cream in his mouth. He kissed her nose, put his arm round her neck.

'I'll wait outside,' said Charlie.

'No!' said Alex, vehemently enough to make her face crease up with pain. 'It's you I want, Charlie. Lawrie Chappell – vamoose. Go and buy coffee. Chat up the night nurses. Whatever. My partner and I need to talk shop.'

Lawrie rolled his eyes. 'I get it. Official business.' He pecked her nose again, then made for the door. 'Actually, I haven't eaten since I left the office. Airline food sucks at the best of times and I didn't exactly have an appetite. You're doing me a favour here, even if I do hate the secrecy. You know what, Charlie? It's tough being married to this one. She asks me how my day was and I say, "Fine. I designed a new pipeline to carry oil through one of the harshest desert environments in the world, and Bob dropped in to say he'll be discussing bonuses next week, and they've got this great new espresso machine on the second floor," and so on and so forth until my poor little petal's eyes are glazing over. And you know what she says when it's finally her turn and I ask her what kind of day *she* had?'

'I don't know, Lawrie. What does she say?'

'She says, "It was okay. If I tell you any more than that, I'll have to shoot you."'

'It's for your own protection, darling,' said Alex. 'And believe me – you wouldn't want to get shot.'

When Lawrie had gone, Charlie perched on the bed. 'How are you really, Alex?' he said. 'Are you just putting on a show for the old man?'

She pressed her hands to her cheeks, then took them away and studied her palms. Charlie wondered what she expected to see there. 'I'm all right, Charlie,' she said, at last. 'It hurts like hell and I'm a bit shaky, but I'm okay. I hate hospitals though. Only other time I was in one was when I gave birth to Fraser. That hurt like hell, too.'

'You'll mend soon enough. Just try and rest.'

'Sod that. I've got too many loose ends flapping round my head. I want you to tell me exactly what we know. I might be lying here like a limp balloon but there's a puzzle to solve here, and you can't do that without me.'

'Bullet missed your modesty gland, too, I see.'

'Shut up and talk.'

'Which do you want? I can't do both.'

'And don't be smart. It doesn't suit you.'

Charlie transferred to the chair beside the bed. He still felt pretty shaky himself. 'All right,' he said, trying to get comfortable on the NHS's idea of a cushion, 'here goes. As I see it, you were way ahead of me right up to the gunshot. You saw the car first – Alex, you saw the *gun* first.'

'Didn't see much after that, though. What happened after I hit the deck?'

'We lost the car. There are enough cameras in the vicinity – we're hoping one of them caught the plate, but there was a lot of traffic, and the rain plays havoc with the focus. All we know for now is it was a black Audi – Brian's got the trace team on it but there's nothing to report yet. Anyway, as soon as I heard the shot, I got Bakker to cover behind his limo, then ran back up the steps to see to you. Our friend Toby hauled Saiki inside like a sack of potatoes. I'm telling you – a president never moved so fast.'

'Good guy, that Toby.'

'I'll second that. The ambulance was incredibly quick – under two minutes. They must have been just round the corner. Once they arrived I let them take over. By that time Johnno and Eric had turned up, and Karen. I tell you, it was good to have back-up. Brian arrived shortly after. Uniform set up SOC tapes, started interviewing Joe and Jane Public. Brian and I checked on Saiki and rostered the embassy staff, and that's when things started getting interesting.'

'Interesting?'

'Yes. The first thing we did was a head-count, made sure everyone was accounted for. And everyone was – except for one.'

'I can't handle suspense in my weakened condition, Charlie.'

'Paul Malamba.'

Her eyes widened. 'Malamba? Really? When did he go?'

'Toby saw him heading out through the back door at ten thirty-five. He didn't say anything at the time – says it was the minister's business, not his. I got Eric to check the phone log from the morning and we found two calls made by Malamba: the first to a 118 number, the second to an establishment in Mayfair called George F. Trumper.'

'The barber shop?'

'That's the one. I called them and asked if they happened to be shaving a tall black man in a natty suit. They told me it was more than their reputation was worth to divulge the identity of their clients. I told them it was a matter of national security. They told me – very politely – to mind my own business. Would you believe I had to fax over my ID before they finally admitted that yes, they did have a man answering Malamba's description in one of their chairs? So I jumped in the car and went straight there.'

'And was he there?'

Charlie laughed. 'You could say that. When I arrived, he was en route to Piccadilly with one half of his face as smooth as a baby's bottom and the other all lathered up with Trumper's Best Sandalwood. You should have seen the look on his face when I nabbed him.'

'I wish I'd been there.'

'Me too, Alex, me too.' Charlie stretched the knots from his back and rasped his hand across the stubble on his chin. Malamba wasn't the only one in need of a shave. 'I don't know what to make of him, Alex, I really don't. Nick Luard still maintains he's a villain, but we can't link him directly to the shooting: his alibi's cast iron. On the other hand, removing himself from the scene barely an hour before the incident took place – and when most of the staff were expecting him to be in the embassy all day...

I mean, how suspicious does he want to make himself look?'

Alex frowned. 'What did you think when you picked him up? Did he seem surprised about what had happened?'

'Not exactly. He said he'd heard about the shooting on the radio, so he knew what was going on. None of the details, though. I'd have to say his reaction seemed pretty genuine. But then we've both commented he's a smooth operator.'

Alex pushed the chocolates aside and eased herself down in the bed, grimacing with each tiny movement. 'I hate being stuck here,' she said. 'The sooner I get out of this place the better. What about Bakker? How did the meeting with Saiki go in the end? It must have been delayed for some time.'

'That's another weird thing. The meeting never happened. While I was seeing to you, Bakker just got back into his limo and drove away. We haven't seen him since.'

Alex shook her head. 'I'm glad we haven't got him under our wing, too. It's hard enough trying to keep these diplomats on the leash without worrying about people like Bakker as well. So what have we got?' She held up her fingers, one at a time. 'Malamba absenting himself from the embassy shortly before someone tries to assassinate the president. Undoubtedly suspicious. Bakker taking to his heels before the gunsmoke's had a chance to clear. Suspicious, but maybe not so much – I mean, who's going to hang around when the bullets are flying?'

'Given Bakker's reputation – and the tip-off we had from Henry Worthington – I still say he's in the frame as a suspect. Is it so hard to assume he's got wind of these plans to nationalise the mines? I'm sure he employs his share of industrial spies. If so, that gives him a pretty good motive to take Saiki down.'

'But he barely avoided getting shot himself.'

'That's one way of looking at it. Another way is that he took a dive on those steps to let the bullet through.'

Alex shook her head. 'I don't buy that. Bakker's a crook, but he isn't crazy.'

Charlie went over to the window. The air, washed clean by the rain, was diamond-clear. Pale lilac sky hung behind the crisp London skyline, like a slowly fading watercolour. 'That storm was a real monster,' he said. 'It was like – you'll laugh at me for saying this – something out of the African plains.'

'It's beautiful now,' said Alex.

'Beautiful, yes.' He closed the blinds.

Someone tapped on the door, then pushed it open without waiting for a reply. It was Lawrie, beaming and balancing three cups of steaming coffee on a tiny tray.

'I brought enough for us all,' he said. 'Mind you, darling, I don't know if you're allowed caffeine on top of your cocktail of painkillers.'

'I'll pass, thanks,' said Alex.

Charlie took his gratefully. He wouldn't get much sleep tonight anyway, not with all this buzzing round his head.

'So, tell me, Charlie,' said Lawrie, throwing himself in the chair Charlie had vacated. 'How's this partner of yours? Is her arse really all it's cracked up to be?'

Charlie glanced at Alex, momentarily confused. Why was Lawrie asking him about his own wife's backside? What could he possibly say to such a question? Then he saw Alex was struggling to suppress a smile.

'Oh, you mean Jackie?' he said, when he finally twigged.

'If it's Jackie who fills out her British Airways uniform with such voluptuousness, why then, yes, I do mean her.'

Avoiding Alex's eye, Charlie fidgeted with

his coffee cup and said, 'I'd hardly call her my partner, Lawrie. We've only had one date – if you can even call two slices of pizza in the Terminal 4 food hall a date.'

'Three dates – you took her to the pictures,' said Alex. 'There were explosions. You said.'

'Explosions?' said Lawrie, raising his eyebrows. 'Really?'

'I don't know what Alex has been telling you,' said Charlie, glaring at her, 'but Jackie and I are just good friends. Now, if you'll excuse me, I really must be getting back.'

Lawrie stood. 'Back to work, or are you done for the day?'

'Well, I'm off duty, if that's what you mean. I think it's the gym for an hour, then home.'

'Still in that little flat in Bayswater?'

'That's the place.'

'Microwave lasagne for supper? Or will it be pizza again?'

Charlie forced a smile. On any other day he'd have responded to Lawrie's ribbing in like spirit. Right now he just wanted to get out of there.

'You look after yourself, Alex,' he said, heading for the door.

'Keep me posted,' she said. 'Let me know if you need help with your arithmetic.'

Charlie nodded, enjoying the puzzled look on Lawrie's face.

'I'll drop in again tomorrow,' he said. 'Sleep well.'

'You too.'

Retracing his steps through the interminable corridors of University College Hospital, with the coffee charging through his veins, Charlie started going over the facts again. Somewhere in this dance of miners and ministers was a crucial step, and they'd missed it.

He reached the lift and thumbed the DOWN button. To his amazement, when the doors opened, the same wizened porter stepped out. Charlie wondered if the old geezer had spent the whole evening riding up and down in the same lift, just waiting for him to return.

'Hello, again,' he said, as they passed each other.

The porter tipped an invisible cap and said, 'How's the nerves, son?'

'Nerves are fine, thanks.'

'Only you look like you've got a lot on your mind.'

'I have.'

The porter winked. 'Sleep on it, lad. It'll all make sense in the morning. Sometimes the answer's staring you in the face.'

'I hope you're right.'

The lift doors slid shut, erasing the porter and the white corridor that was his home. Charlie closed his eyes, let the pieces of the puzzle spin round his head and waited for everything to fall into place.

13

June 26th

19:58

Cabinet Office, Whitehall

'Look, Henry, I'm not trying to push you into saying anything you don't want to say – if I don't know by now what a tight-lipped bastard you can be when you want to I must be a pretty poor judge of character – it's just that this time it's more than a newspaper headline I'm after: we're talking about my whole life here. My whole fucking life's on the line, Henry, and you're the only friend I've got on the inside track. The only one. All I'm asking is you give me a clue. You can be vague, you can be sketchy – for God's sake, I'll even promise not to publish it – just put me out of my misery, please.'

'Misery is what you put dogs out of, Jack,' said Henry. 'I'm sorry, but I don't think I can help.'

Jack sneezed down the phone.

'Fucking hay fever. Look, Henry – I'm not calling you in my capacity as celebrated newspaper hack – I'm your brother-in-law, for God's sake. I just want to know who you think tried to bump off Mani Saiki this morning. Strictly off the record. Is that too much to ask?'

'For the last time, Jack, I can't tell you what theories SODs are following up because I don't know myself. You know the players in this game as well as I do. I'm sure you'll get just as much joy working it out for yourself.'

'Precious little joy in all this, Henry, I'll tell you that much for nothing. And I'll tell you something else: if you were in my shoes you'd see things differently. First thing this morning I tell you Piet Bakker's after my blood, then a couple of hours later I find out he's mixed up in a shooting in central London. Can you blame me for being worried?'

'Just because Bakker was present at the incident,' Henry replied, 'doesn't mean he was involved with the assassination attempt.'

'So you're saying it had nothing to do with him? Then who the hell was it, Henry?'

'I'm not saying anything of the sort, and

174

you know it. I'm just saying you're jumping to conclusions. If I were you, I'd…'

'Where's Bakker now?'

'What?'

'Where is he now? According to the *Standard*, right after the shooting he jumped in his car and took off. So where did he go? Is he still on the loose? Have they picked him up yet?'

'Jack, you know I can't discuss the details of the case.'

'You can at least tell me where Bakker is.'

'You're talking about a material witness in an attempted homicide. I can't tell you anything and you know it.' *And anyway, I don't bloody well know myself.*

The truth was Piet Bakker was still at large. He'd abandoned the scene even before the ambulance had turned up. In Henry's opinion that made him guilty as hell. Bakker was on the run, no doubt about it – probably out of the country already. He'd arrived in a private jet; it wouldn't be hard for him to arrange an equally discreet departure.

Part of him wanted to share this suspicion with Jack, to convince him that his fears of reprisal for the libellous newspaper articles were just paranoia. The last thing on Bakker's mind now would be some Fleet Street terrier snapping at his heels: he'd be more concerned about British security unleashing the hounds.

What stopped him – apart from not wanting to admit that he too was in the dark – was sure knowledge that when you were talking to Jack McClintock there was no such thing as 'off the record'.

'If you won't talk about Bakker,' said Jack, 'at least tell me about Paul Malamba.'

Henry's arm had been sagging, pulling the phone further and further from his ear. Now he sat up, pulled the handset close again. 'Why are you interested in Malamba?' he said, as casually as he could manage.

Jack hesitated. 'All right, Henry, I'll do you a favour. Keep you in the loop, even if you're determined to keep me out of it. One of our junior reporters happened to be walking down Curzon Street at lunch-time today when a red BMW came tearing round the corner and pulled up by the kerb. An officer jumped out and apprehended a tall black man who'd just left that fancy barber shop – Trumper. Despite the fact he was still half-covered in shaving foam, his description matches that of the Republic of Limpopo Minister for Minerals. This will all be in *The Times* tomorrow, by the way. Makes a

176

change for me to be giving you the scoop, doesn't it?'

'Will it really be in the paper, Jack?' said Henry. 'Are you sure you want to go out on a limb again?' He suddenly felt very tired. The carriage clock on the marble mantel told him eight o'clock had come and gone, which made this officially Another Late Night. His in-tray was still piled with briefs he had to read before the morning; his email inbox was full of messages highlighted bold for Unread and flagged High Priority. He really didn't need this.

Again there was silence on the line. 'Whether we use the article or not,' Jack said, at last, 'it can't do any harm to tell me if it was Malamba. I called Trumper but they're a bunch of tight-lipped bastards – anyone would think they were a Masonic Lodge. I didn't tell them I was a journalist, but I think they guessed.'

'I wonder how,' murmured Henry. But Jack was in full flow.

'They told me their clients relied on their discretion. I asked them what their view was on the freedom of the press and d'you know what they told me? They told me they'd been adhering to the Data Protection Act a hundred years before it even existed. Can

177

you believe it?'

'Actually,' said Henry, keen to keep the conversation off the subject of Paul Malamba, 'I can. They've been protecting the secrets of the aristocracy since before you or I were born.'

Jack sneezed again. 'All this stress is making my hay fever worse, Henry, and it's your fault. Help me out here – just give me a few hard facts. That's all I need. Then I'll sleep easier knowing me and Mary and the kids are safe.'

That last line hit Henry harder than any other words Jack McClintock's whining voice had delivered. It was that emotional Joker again, the one card guaranteed to have Henry cashing in his conversational chips.

'It seems to me that facts have been pretty hard to come by all round, Jack,' he said. 'In the interests of national security, I'll ask you again: what do you know about the so-called "British connection" that enabled Kissonga to siphon all that money out of his country? And while you're at it, you can tell me how you came by such sensitive information. Who's the stool pigeon, Jack? What's your source?'

The sneezing stopped. The carriage clock ticked through the silence. Henry waited, held his breath.

'I don't think we've got anything else to say to each other,' said Jack.

The line went dead.

14

June 26th

22:13

MI6 Headquarters

Malamba resisted the urge to get up and walk round the room. There would be cameras everywhere, tracking his every move. That was exactly why Luard had left him alone: to see what he would do. Well, he would confound them by doing nothing. He would sit quietly with his hands in his lap. He would wait. Let them make of that what they would.

Less than five minutes passed before he felt compelled to check the time. It was past ten. This day was going on forever. He looked closer at his Rolex. There was a scratch on the glass. When had that happened? When he had been shoved into the back of Paddon's BMW, he suspected. At the time he had not understood why the SODs officer had been so enraged. Now he did.

Somebody shot his partner, he thought. *No wonder he was angry.*

He supposed he should feel angry himself. Detained first by the British police, and now by their security service. So much for diplomatic immunity. But, though he searched for it, there was no anger inside him. Only concern. This visit was falling apart. The edifice he was constructing was beginning to look like a house of cards.

He had spent the afternoon at New Scotland Yard. Not in a cell, nor even exactly in custody. But the interview had lasted a very long time. The man in charge of the SODs division – a short, dour man called Brian Burfield – had asked him endless questions about his movements that morning, forcing him to repeat himself again and again. What conversations had he had with Saiki? Why had he left through the back door? Burfield seemed particularly interested in what he had bought in the Soho shop – halfway through this a junior officer had brought in the bag of records he had left behind at Trumper. Burfield had counted out the vinyls one at a time, as if hoping to catch Malamba out.

Burfield had asked him constantly if he

wanted a solicitor present. Each time Malamba had declined, even though he knew he
should at least have someone brought over
from the embassy. This was not his country
and without proper support he was vulner-
able. Each time he refused, Burfield grew
increasingly uncomfortable. Perversely,
Malamba found that satisfying.

Besides, what could they charge him with?
His tracks were clean.

All the same, he was glad when they finally
gave up and drove him back to the hotel.
President Saiki would join him later, they
said. It was likely their visit to the United
Kingdom would be cut short. Perhaps he
would like to spend the evening packing his
bags?

They had posted a guard outside the suite
– not Paddon this time, but one of his
colleagues, a great bear of a man called Johnson. Malamba ordered room service. When
the meal arrived (filet mignon, rare), he took
the tray to the desk and worked through a
flood of emails on his laptop while he ate.
Thanks to his inbox filters, at the top of the
electronic pile was a message from Alice.

*Honey, they told me about the shooting. They tell
me not to worry but you know I do. Finish what*

you have to do and call me when your job there is done. We will see each other again soon, where we arranged. I love you. Your Always Alice.

'Always Alice'. It was the nickname he had given her the day they had met, on a crowded bus in Limpopo City. He was newly graduated, having just returned from his studies in England, and his eyes were full of the future. When the big girl on the bus sat next to him and offered to share her Coke, she became part of his outlook, too.

'Please, do not go,' he had said when the bus reached her stop.

'This is the school where I work,' she replied. 'If you make me stay on this bus, you will deprive the Republic's children of a proper education.'

'Will I see you again?'

'Same bus, same time, every day. Always the same.'

'What is your name?'

'That never changes either. Alice. It is always Alice.'

Alice – do not worry. I am perfectly well, and so is Mani. I am sure the British security people will clear up all this confusion very quickly. I hope to conclude my business here very quickly,

183

after which we will be together again.
He thought for a moment, then added:
I could not do any of this without you. I love you always. Paul.

He clicked Send.

Malamba had barely finished his steak – and dealt with less than half his emails – when Sergeant Johnson showed in a tall, skinny man. Malamba's first thought was *hotel management* – the man was looking round the suite as if he owned it. But he and Saiki had been introduced to all the senior staff on their arrival, and this man had not been among them. Nor did he look like the kind of man with whom you could negotiate a room rate discount

'Good evening, Mr Malamba,' said the man when the SODs officer had left. He handed over a leather wallet with an ID card inside. Malamba inspected the ID, which identified the man as Nicholas Luard. Not only did he work for the British security service, it appeared that he ran a rather large part of it.

'I have of course heard of MI6,' said Malamba, handing back the wallet. 'I am puzzled as to why they should have heard of me. I am especially puzzled because the identity card says you are the man in charge. Do you not have people to run your errands for you?'

The thin man flashed a thin smile. 'Sometimes the personal touch is required. Mr Malamba, I would like you to come with me, please.'

'Where?'

'To my office.'

'Why?'

'There are a number of matters I would like to discuss with you.'

'Am I to be interrogated?'

'You are free to accept or decline my invitation, as you see fit. I am not in a position to force you to do anything against your will. I can assure you that MI6 will respect your diplomatic status at all times.'

'Then I refuse.'

'As is your right. However...' Luard strolled to the bureau where Malamba had been working. Malamba tensed – his laptop was open, his email inbox in plain view. Luard reached over the bureau to the wall, where a framed print of Wren's drawing of St Paul's Cathedral was hanging askew, and straightened the picture. '...when I tell you what I would like to discuss, you might change your mind.'

Malamba crossed the room and closed his laptop. 'Why would I do that?'

'Because, amongst other things, I want to talk to you about your relationship with Piet Bakker.'

That made Malamba hesitate.

He liked to believe he could get on with almost anyone. It was a politician's art, but it was more than that: it was simply the way he was. But this man ... he made Malamba's skin want to curl off his back and shrivel on the floor. He wanted to back away, to tell him to leave the room, just get out.

And yet...

How much did British Intelligence really know about Piet Bakker? More to the point, how much did they know about him, Paul Malamba? If they really did suspect he was behind today's assassination attempt, would they assume he was also behind the bombing of the bridge back in the Republic of Limpopo? He had to find out what they knew. The only way of doing that was to talk to them.

'I will come with you,' he said, slowly, 'as long as I can ask you a question first.'

'Ask away.'

'Do you have what they call "double-oh" status?'

Luard's thin smile became the generous grin of a mako shark. 'My dear Mr Malamba – I think you've been reading too much Ian Fleming.'

No sooner had Luard shown Malamba into the interview room than he had excused himself.

'I'll be back in ten minutes,' he said. 'I have a few things I must attend to before we start. Would you like a cup of tea? Coffee, perhaps?'

'Coffee, please,' said Malamba. 'Black, one sugar.'

Ten minutes, thought Malamba. *Long enough for me to fidget and start poking around. Long enough for me to sweat a little.*

The room was cleverly arranged. It was very light – three of the walls were glass partitions opening into other offices. It was the antithesis of a holding cell: an airy, transparent space in which nothing could possibly be concealed. No prisoner could be mistreated in such a room, because everyone would see.

Yet, when you looked carefully, you found the sight-lines into the other offices were not as unbroken as they appeared. Moreover, the offices were partitioned off with frosted screens; the people in them were just shadow puppets. The longer he sat here, the more Malamba realised he could not really see anybody else at all ... and nobody else could see him.

The mirror on the solid fourth wall was probably two-way, with an observation room behind. This room, with its terracotta carpet, its brushed-steel furniture and its glass walls might look like an architect's dream, but was an interrogation cell all the same.

The door whispered open. Luard entered carrying two polystyrene cups. Tucked under his arm was a thin manila folder.

'I'm sorry, I had to get these from the machine,' he said, placing both cups and folder on the glass-topped table. 'There's not much choice at this time of night.'

Do you really expect me to believe MI6 slows down when it gets dark? 'I understand,' said Malamba. 'Instant coffee is perfectly acceptable, thank you.'

'You might not think that when you've tasted it.'

Malamba tasted it and Luard was right, it was awful. But he smiled and said it was delicious, and the other man's expression told him he knew it was a lie.

'So,' said Malamba. 'You said you wanted

to talk about Piet Bakker. Where would you like to start?'

Luard pulled one of the leather-and-steel chairs round from the other side of the table and positioned it beside Malamba's. 'Let's not have barriers here, Mr Malamba. I want us to talk like two old friends having drinks beside the fire.'

Malamba made a show of looking round the room. 'I see no fire, Mr Luard. And we are drinking cheap coffee, not brandy. But I understand the sentiment.'

'Quite.' Again the thin smile, this time very brief. 'I will come to Mr Bakker, but first I wanted to talk about the events of this afternoon.'

Malamba steepled his fingers. 'I have already discussed the shooting at great length with Chief Superintendent Burfield at New Scotland Yard. As you must know, at the time of the incident I was in a barber's chair being shaved. Do you really expect me to go through it all again?'

'It's not the incident itself I want to discuss. It's just that ... well, a man in your position might stand to gain a great deal if one of these assassination attempts were to succeed.'

'I do not know what you mean.'

'Come now, Mr Malamba. Your face is almost as well-known in your country as that of your president. Half of the Republic of Limpopo's men want you to lead them to economic independence and half the women want you in their beds.'

Malamba grasped the arms of the chair and rose from his seat. Here was the anger that had eluded him. 'How dare you! I did not come here to be...'

'Calm down, Mr Malamba. I am merely pointing out that you are Mani Saiki's natural successor and a popular figure. Surely you understand that some people might see that as a motive for wanting him dead.'

Malamba hovered, still halfway to his feet. 'Including MI6?'

Luard shrugged. It was a hateful gesture that showed he considered himself superior to Malamba. *He probably feels superior to everyone*, Malamba thought. As a long-time chess player he had learned that every opponent had a weakness, if you can but seek it out. Luard's weakness was his arrogance.

'I am not saying I believe you were behind it,' said Luard, as Malamba slowly sat down again. 'I merely point out the facts as they might appear. Although...'

'Although what?'

Luard picked up the folder and flipped it open. He leafed through several sheets of flimsy paper – they were almost like onion-skins – before stopping at one in particular. 'Earlier today I spoke to a gentleman of your acquaintance: one James Fenchurch. I believe you roomed together at York University. One of the banking dynasty, is our James Jr. You do move in high circles, don't you, Mr Malamba?'

'You have been speaking to Jimmy?' Malamba's anger was replaced by simple astonishment. Where on earth was this leading?

'Your friend and heir to untold millions told me that your ambition was to be President of the Republic. In fact, yes, here we are ... on one occasion you said, "Wait until I get my hands on that country. Then I'll show the world what I am made of."' Luard lowered the folder and raised his eyebrows. 'Do you have any comment on that, Mr Malamba?'

'That was over twenty years ago,' said Malamba. His lips moved but his teeth did not. If he opened his jaws he was likely to bury them in Nick Luard's neck. 'Did you not have dreams when you were young, Mr Luard? Perhaps you dreamed of being James Bond, of carrying a gun and shooting the villain just as he is about to plant a bullet in the heroine's chest. Is it as exciting as you had hoped, the intelligence game? Or is it all just one long day at the office? Do you ever wonder where are the cars and the girls and the gadgets?'

He thought that might have struck home. But Luard's gaunt face was hard to read.

'Perhaps we should move on to the subject of Piet Bakker,' Luard said, curtly. 'It is, after all, why I invited you here tonight.'

'Invited? I wonder if I really had a choice. Is this conversation being recorded, by the way?'

'Please, Mr Malamba, we can get through this much more quickly if you cooperate.'

'Then let us get through it. Ask your questions. If I can help you, I shall. If not ... I have a lot of work to do.'

'How long did you work for Bakker Diamonds and Minerals?'

'Twenty-one years. Why do you ask me this? My employment history is common knowledge. I have nothing to hide.'

Luard went on. 'You reached the position of General Manager after just two years with the company – a meteoric rise by anybody's standards.'

'Bakker liked the way I operated. I was

good with people. He was not – by his own admission, I should add. Piet Bakker had his faults, but to his credit, he was always ready to acknowledge them.'

'I'm interested to hear you talk about him in the past tense.'

Malamba frowned. 'We are talking about the past, are we not? You must forgive me – English is not my first language.'

Luard stared at him for a moment before continuing. 'As the years went by, would it be fair to say Bakker relied on you more and more when it came to dealing with, shall we say, sensitive staffing issues?'

'I do not know what you mean.'

'Personnel issues, industrial action, that kind of thing. And, modest as you are, you must know your English is, in fact, very good. As is...' he consulted the folder again '...your French, German and, recently, Japanese. Which is why Bakker took you with him on so many of his foreign trips.'

'My job took me to other countries, including many outside the African continent. Mining is a global business, Mr Luard. Travel is necessary.'

Malamba wondered where Luard was going with this. He felt like a witness in the stand, being led down a carefully plotted path by a clever barrister. At the end of the path would be a trap, primed and ready to be sprung.

'Of course. And what an excellent grounding for a career in international politics.'

'Indeed.'

'Your years at York University must have given you a particular affinity with the United Kingdom.'

'I have much affection for these islands.'

'You like our beer.'

'The warmer the better.'

'And you really do speak our language very well.'

'You flatter me.'

'So it was only natural that Bakker included you in all his dealings with his British friends, wasn't it?'

Malamba heard the spring of the trap in his head. But he was ready for it. He pasted a smile on his face and said, 'I am afraid I do not know what you mean. What British friends are you talking about?' He saw his own smile reflected in Luard's face and added, 'Tell me, Mr Luard – do you play chess?'

'As a matter of fact, I do. How did you know?'

'It was just a wild guess.'

Luard sat back in his chair. He picked up one of the polystyrene cups and pushed the other towards Malamba. 'You should drink this before it gets cold.'

'Oh,' said Malamba, 'I do not think I will be here long enough for that. Do you?'

Seeing Luard scowl – however briefly – was the most satisfying moment Malamba had had all day. It was a small victory, like taking a pawn. But, as Alice was always reminding him, it is sometimes the small victories that make the big differences.

Luard drank his coffee in three long gulps. He pulled his chair round to face Malamba and leaned forward with his elbows on his knees and his hands dangling down. 'I've said all along there's more to you than meets the eye. Don't think you've fooled me, because you haven't – not for a moment. I don't know what kind of deal you're cooking up with Bakker, but I do believe it's connected to all that money that he and Kissonga siphoned out of the Republic. But do you know what? I think you're out of your depth. Whatever game it is you're playing, I think you've discovered there's more at stake than you ever realised.'

'You are crazy,' said Malamba. 'There is no deal. There is no game.'

'And do you know what else I think? I think that as long as you're dealing with Bakker, you're doing it in the shadow of Steven's gravestone. And you can't stand it. Because that's what's really behind all this, isn't it, Mr Malamba? Revenge for your brother's death. The trouble is, the desire for revenge has robbed you of the ability to choose between right and wrong. You're not the innocent everyone thinks you are. There may be a good guy in all of this – although personally I doubt it – but one thing's for certain: it isn't you.'

The second half of this speech washed over Malamba like a bitter tide. As soon as Luard mentioned his brother's name, he felt his fists bunch, felt himself lurch forward in the chair. The anger was back, only now it was red rage rising through him like lava, molten rock ready to spill out into this slick glass room, spill over the man who might just as well have been shining a spotlight in his face while his colleagues behind the one-way mirror aimed their cameras and prepared the thumbscrews.

He took a breath, held it, let it out. Slowly he straightened his fingers, let his body relax back into the chair. Luard was watching him closely with no sign of fear, only curiosity.

Well, Paul Malamba could match him for coldness any day.

'You are wrong,' he said, enunciating each word carefully and slowly. 'And if tomorrow's events play themselves out according to plan, you will find out just how far from the truth you are.' He stood. Far beyond the glass walls of the interview room, his many reflections stood, too. 'And now, I request that you honour my diplomatic status and return me to my hotel.'

Luard's eyes looked first at him, then through him, towards the mirror.

'I will escort you personally, minister,' he said, 'just as soon as the time comes for you to leave. After all, we wouldn't want anything to happen to you. Before then, however, there are just a few more things I'd like to discuss.'

15

June 27th

09:37

Carlton House Terrace

Charlie should have felt comfortable with Sergeant Jeff Johnson at his side. Johnno was almost as wide as he was tall and looked as if he'd been built from bricks. Like Charlie, he'd served in the Met before being transferred to SODs. Before the Met he'd been an infantryman. That in itself was a rarity; he was also the only ex-soldier Charlie had met who actually thought policing was tougher than wearing khaki.

'Now I ain't sayin' the Gulf was a cakewalk,' he told Charlie once. 'No, sir. All I'm sayin' is, on a gig like that, you're there to take orders. They tell you what to do and you say, "Yessir," and you do it. If you can avoid armour-piercing rounds along the way, all the better. Being a cop – that's a whole different ball game.'

Johnno's father was from Boston, which accounted for his transatlantic drawl and his inexplicable love of pancakes. His squaddie crew cut and the long scar on his cheek made him a formidable presence out on patrol – people rarely gave him any lip – but Charlie couldn't help wishing it was Alex at his side.

Would you have thrown yourself in front of that bullet? he wondered, as Johnno took up his position outside the meeting-room door. Perhaps. But only if he'd been ordered to.

'Anything I need to know?' asked Johnno. He held his MP5 submachine gun as if it were a toy. Legend said that, when his patrol car had suffered the embarrassing combination of a blown-out tyre and a missing jack, he'd held it up by the bumper while his partner changed the wheel.

'All's quiet so far,' said Charlie. 'Saiki and Malamba arrived together about half-an-hour ago. They're in there now with the Foreign Secretary.' He nodded towards the door. 'Saiki was bright as a button – you wouldn't think yesterday he'd been dicing with death.'

'What about the other guy? The chief said he spent time with the spooks last night.'

'Same as ever. Neatly pressed and smooth as you like. A bit tired, maybe, but then he was late to bed.'

Johnno looked both ways along the corridor. 'Well, nobody's gettin' past me. You gonna do your rounds?'

'Yes. It's only really the foyer I'm worried about – the rest of this place is sealed up pretty tight. Give me fifteen minutes or so. They won't be out of there before eleven anyway. Just sit tight and stay sharp.'

'Sure thing, boss. You know me – ready for anything.'

If Alex went to Dubai with Lawrie, there was a good chance Johnno would be his new partner. Charlie tried to imagine spending long hours in the BMW with this drawling mountain of muscle. He'd have to get used to eating donuts and having an opinion on the latest Red Sox scores. Plus, elbow room would be an issue. He wasn't sure he was ready for it.

He made his way down the corridor to the main staircase. Carlton House Terrace felt a little like a hotel that was once plush, but was now going to seed. The expensive carpets were frayed; the woodwork was shiny with age rather than polish. Still, security was good, with swipe-card locks on all the connecting doors and cameras at every turn. With so many corridors, and so many turns, that meant a lot of cameras.

Despite the events of yesterday, things had – to all intents and purposes – returned to normal. Saiki and Malamba's meeting with the Foreign Secretary was part of their original schedule. However, Charlie suspected the actual agenda of the meeting might have been revised a little following the incident at the embassy. The word was this whole visit would be wrapped up as quickly as possible, and the two gentlemen from the Republic of Limpopo hustled out of the country on the earliest available flight. The next stop on their tour was due to be Washington DC; no doubt the Americans would be more than happy to welcome their African guests a few days early.

As he descended the wide, curving staircase, Charlie wondered what Nick Luard had said to Malamba at MI6 headquarters last night. He thought back to Luard's comments at that briefing session they'd had at Scotland Yard. What was it he'd said? *There's more to Paul Malamba than meets the eye.*

After a few days shadowing the man, Charlie thought the same. Contrarily, he also thought Nick Luard was full of shit.

The truth lay somewhere in the middle.

The foyer was clear. At Charlie's request, they'd posted extra security at the main door. Everyone was relaxed and alert. He chatted briefly with the receptionist, checked the side doors himself, then walked out into the middle of the foyer. He stood there under the high ceiling, listening to distant footsteps and warbling phones. Over the low rumble of the traffic, very faint, he could hear the sound of roadworks.

All quiet. No hunches, nothing on the radar. Good. He'd seen enough blood for one week.

He pulled out his mobile, called Alex. She picked up on the first ring.

'Hey,' he said, 'where are you?'

'Still in my hospital bed, worse luck. But the scuttlebutt is they're letting me out this afternoon. I'm just waiting for the doctors to do their rounds.'

'Should you be using your phone in there?'

'New policy.' He could almost see her *whatever* shrug. 'Anyway, what are they going to do – arrest me?'

'So you'll be at home later on?'

'I'd bloody better be.'

'I'll come round. If that's okay.'

'Of course it is. I've got a vested interest in this case, Charlie Paddon. Now more than ever. I need you to keep me in the loop. More chocolate wouldn't go amiss, either.'

The mobile's ringtone chimed through her voice. Charlie checked the screen; it was a Whitehall number. 'Alex – gotta go. Duty calls. Keep your knickers clean.'

'In this place that's harder than it looks. See you later.'

Charlie ended the call and switched lines. 'Brian?' he said. 'What's the latest?'

'I'm in Henry Worthington's office,' said Brian. He sounded tense, which made Charlie's ears prick up. Whenever Brian called from Whitehall he usually just sounded glum. 'Luard's here, and Henry, of course. I need you here now. Emergency meeting.'

What emergency? 'You're sure you need me right now, Brian? I mean, I'm supposed to be looking after...'

'Ten minutes, Charlie. Better still, five.' And he hung up.

It took Charlie two minutes to get to the car and another two to manoeuvre his way round the van delivering frozen food to the Carlton House canteen. As he nudged the BMW between a set of bollards and the van's front wing, he called Johnno.

'Just sit tight. Call me if anything happens.'

'You want me to call you, or deal with the somethin' that's happenin'?'

'Sarcasm doesn't suit you. Just don't shoot anyone who looks important.'

'Aw, you take the fun out of the job. So what's the crisis?'

'I'll tell you when I know. The fact they're pulling me out means they must think Saiki's safe for now.'

'Easy for them to say.'

'My feelings exactly.'

Trafalgar Square was gridlocked as usual. Charlie tried to steer through the usual mess of buses, cabs and businessmen with off-roaders and enough money to swallow the congestion charge without blinking. On top of that there were two coaches dumping schoolchildren outside the National Gallery and some kind of art installation being erected around the base Nelson's Column. As far as Charlie could remember from the news, it was a controversial performance piece because the artist was planning to be buried underground for two months, while being visible to the public through a viewing panel. Charlie suspected the novelty would wear off on the first Saturday night when the twentieth stag party rolled over to have a look.

He travelled fifty metres before the traffic set like concrete, at which point he lit the blues and broke a hole in it. A line of cabs peeled on to the kerb like synchronised swimmers, scattering the tourists who stared open-mouthed at the red BMW battering its way round London's most famous monument. Distracted, a member of the burial team let go of one end of a steel coffin, and another gesticulated wildly. A mushroom cloud of pigeons burst into the sky.

'Don't blame me,' said Charlie, under his breath. 'I'm only following orders.'

Parking at Whitehall was no easier than it had been at Carlton House Terrace. The drains were up, and getting past the men with their yellow jackets and machinery proved, ultimately, impossible. He slewed the BMW at an angle between the site hut and the Portaloo and stormed into the building. By the time he reached Henry Worthington's office he felt ready to hit someone.

Outside the door he paused, took a deep breath. Behind her desk, Worthington's PA gave him a knowing smile.

'Go on in,' she said. 'They're waiting for you.' She dropped him a wink, which helped lower his temperature to the point where he could enter without taking the door off its hinges.

They were sat waiting, the three of them, drinking coffee. Brian looked as tense as he'd sounded on the phone – so did Worthington, for that matter. Luard just looked his usual supercilious self.

'Glad you're here, Charlie,' said Brian.

'I wish I could say the same.' There, it was out. Ah well, in for a penny... 'Brian – what the hell is so important that it takes me off the front line where I'm supposed to be guarding a foreign president with a nasty history of assassination attempts? Johnno's good but one body's just not enough. Even one as big as his. If they come for Saiki now we get more than egg on our faces. We fail in our basic duty. Worse than that – we let these people down.'

Brian said nothing, simply raised his hand. Charlie knew the gesture – and the expression that accompanied it. He shut up.

'At two thirty-one this morning,' he said, 'a police constable was on routine patrol round the perimeter of Green Park when she discovered what she thought at first was a heap of clothes. On closer inspection it turned out to be the body of a man in his mid-fifties. The man's throat had been cut with what we believe to be a common-or-garden steak knife. He bled to death some time in the small hours.' He paused. 'We have since confirmed the identity of the man as Piet Rudi Bakker, president and CEO of Bakker Diamonds and Minerals of Johannesburg, South Africa.'

16

June 27th

10:13

Cabinet Office, Whitehall

Brian Burfield began by showing Paddon the scene-of-crime pictures. Henry let them get on with it. He'd looked at the top two pictures and handed them straight back. Pictures of an ugly man with staring eyes and a slashed throat were not what he wanted to see before lunch. Or at all, for that matter.

'What's the situation with the press?' asked Paddon, as he studied the photos.

'What do you mean?' said Henry. He had half an eye on the phone. It would be just his luck for Jack to call in the middle of this meeting. If he did, what could he say?

'I mean, have they got hold of this story yet? Given their excitement over yesterday's shooting, Bakker's death is going to start a feeding frenzy.'

'So far we've managed to suppress it. Isn't that right, Brian?'

'Yes,' said Burfield. 'We were lucky twice over. First the body was found by a beat officer. Second, that beat officer recognised Bakker and called it straight into the Foreign Office. We had double-shift forensics down there faster than you can spit. Performed a fingertip search as it was getting light, got out while the first joggers were still eating their Weetabix. It was quite an operation. You'd never know we were there.'

Paddon raised his eyebrows. 'Not exactly out of the manual.'

'Forget the manual,' said Henry. 'If sticking to the manual means people getting shot in the head or having their throats cut, I suggest we throw the manual away.' Henry fixed them all, one by one, with his best Whitehall glare. 'Gentleman, this is in every respect a massive embarrassment both for your individual departments and for Her Majesty's Government. A leading South African industrialist – and let's forget the fact that the man's practically a gangster for a moment, we're talking about the eyes of the world here – has been murdered just round the corner from Buckingham Palace.

Frankly, I wouldn't care if the press never got hold of this one. Unfortunately the chances of that are slim. I just wonder what it will do for our reputation – our *nation's* reputation – when it does get out.'

Outside the window, the drills seemed to have bred. What the hell were they doing down there? Extending the Underground? Henry raised his voice over the racket.

'People like Piet Bakker – and foreign leaders like Mani Saiki – come to Great Britain to do business because they believe they will be looked after here. They believe this is a civilised country, somewhere safe to do business. We represent everything they aspire to.' He paused. 'It only takes one sleazy murder in a London park to change all that. To make people afraid it might happen to them.'

'Murder happens everywhere,' said Paddon. 'We can only do our best.'

'This time it seems your best wasn't good enough.'

Henry watched with satisfaction as Paddon bit back a retort. It was unfair to have a go, he supposed. After all, SODs hadn't been responsible for Bakker's safety. And he had just dragged Paddon away from his post. Still, it didn't hurt for the plods to

210

know their place.

'We'll find the killer,' said Burfield. 'And for the record, Henry, we didn't process the scene quickly to dodge the press. We did it because Saiki's still at risk. There are a lot of wheels turning here. Once we've got the killer they can have all the headlines they want.'

'Welcome aboard, Brian,' said Luard, from the corner. 'We'll make an intelligent man of you yet.'

'I think you mean "intelligence man", Nick,' said Henry. 'On the subject of which, I'm surprised MI6 didn't get a sniff of this. You had plenty of theories about Piet Bakker a few days ago, Nick. Surely you can bring something to the party?'

Nick Luard started his usual preen-and-waffle routine. Henry tuned out – the MI6 man had arrived early; he'd heard all this before. He couldn't stop thinking about Jack. Eileen was holding his regular calls but there was still his alpha direct line – what Jack McClintock called the 'bat-phone'. He could, theoretically, bar calls on even that; unfortunately, the Prime Minister wouldn't be impressed if he took it into his head to call Henry Worthington direct and found himself listening to 'Dancing Queen'.

Why, oh why, had he ever given Jack that number? It was useful enough having a tame hack to mop up his deliberate leaks, quite another having the man Fleet Street called Jack Russell worrying his ankles every verse end. Jack had spent half of yesterday grilling him about Bakker's whereabouts. The fact he hadn't called yet this morning only meant he was building up for a broadside.

Under normal circumstance he'd have been able to deal with it. Henry was used to deflecting people. Especially journalists, and especially Jack. But this was different, and the reason for that was standing right in front of him: the photograph of his nephews and the rainbow trout. Tim and Jason, looking like they would live forever.

If Jack called, could he really not tell him Bakker was dead? If he did, and Jack scooped the story on to the front page of *The Times*, it would be a hard one for Henry to spin his way out of. Not for the first time, he started thinking seriously about somewhere very warm, with a very golden, very private beach.

Luard was still droning on. *Any minute now he'll mention the big picture.*

'...but if we think about the big picture...'

Luard obliged; Henry grimaced '...it should come as no surprise to us that Bakker died the way he did. He had plenty of enemies. I could show you a stack of files about his various business activities; a lot of them would make your hair curl. If you want my opinion, I would say Piet Bakker simply died as he lived: in the shadows and on the edge of the law. However, given the proximity of the crime scene to the Charles Darwin, I think we can all agree which way the wind appears to be blowing.'

'Helpful as ever, Nick,' said Henry. 'It's back to you, Brian. Are there any concrete leads you can share with us before we go and break the news to President Saiki?'

'It's early days,' said Burfield. Now it was Luard's turn to snort. Henry briefly considered giving them duelling pistols. 'We know the killer was right-handed and very strong. Direction of the stroke and the depth of the cut tell us that. Unfortunately the murder weapon was removed from the scene; frankly, I don't think we'll find it until we find the killer. Of course it could already be at the bottom of the Thames. Apart from the fatal wound, the victim was unharmed.'

'So we're assuming he was in the park at the time?' said Paddon.

'No evidence to the contrary,' said Burfield. 'Not yet.'

'Bakker Diamonds and Minerals have an office in Mayfair,' said Luard, consulting a folder of his own. 'And Bakker keeps an apartment near Marble Arch and another in, let me see, Hammersmith.'

'That could fit – walking back to his digs after an evening pushing paper,' grunted Burfield. 'Just like you, Henry.'

'He could have been meeting someone in the park,' said Paddon.

'Perhaps he was cruising,' smirked Luard.

'Well, whatever his reason for being there,' said Henry hastily, 'the main thing is he *was* there. Is there anything else, Brian? Could it have been a mugging gone wrong?'

'Not likely,' said Burfield. 'On the body we found a wallet containing six credit cards and over two thousand pounds Sterling, plus the usual keys, mobile phone et cetera. No attempt at robbery. It was murder, pure and simple.'

Charlie Paddon's fingers were tapping lightly on the arms of the chair. He looked impatient, anxious to get moving. Henry was surprised to find he felt the same. Usually he preferred the view from his desk, but today it wasn't enough. Perhaps it was time to roll up his sleeves and get his hands dirty.

With a barely-disguised shiver, he recalled the last time he'd felt this way. It was back in March, when the SODs had managed to lose the Croatian Foreign Minister. He'd stepped in then, flying all the way to Edinburgh to help resolve the situation. There had been a lot of shit hitting the fan that day, and it had taken all Henry's guile to keep it from sticking to the department walls. In particular, to Henry Worthington.

Was he about to go through all that again?

'I think we've covered everything, gentlemen,' he said. 'Now I really think we should get moving. I want to intercept President Saiki before he moves on to his next meeting.'

'How do you think he'll react?' said Charlie, as they made ready to leave.

'He'll jump for joy,' said Burfield. Everyone stared at him. 'Him and Malamba both. Why wouldn't they? Bakker was the thorn in their side. Nothing to stop them taking his mines now. They do that, they're national heroes. In one respect I agree with Nick – it's a hell of a motive.'

'Do you really believe the President of the Republic of Limpopo would resort to murder just to complete a political process?'

said Henry, genuinely astonished. He was even more astonished by the sight of these two old adversaries being on the same side for once.

Burfield shrugged. 'Just stating facts, Henry. The damage you'd do with press releases and negative spin, these boys do with a knife. Same end result. The truth will out I'm sure. Then we'll know.' He picked up the case folder. One of the SOC photos slipped out, revealing for a second time Piet Bakker's slashed throat. It was a large photo taken at high resolution, in full colour.

Henry looked away. His eyes went straight to the picture of Tim and Jason. Even if Jack had good grounds for feeling paranoid, with Bakker dead the boys were surely safe.

Weren't they?

17

June 27th

11:25

Carlton House Terrace

Important as the meeting was, Paul Malamba found it hard to keep his mind on the agenda. He was tired for a start; also, the British Foreign Secretary spoke in what could only be described as a monotone. The Foreign Secretary's name was Vincent Ploughman, but he was known both to Parliament and the world at large as the 'Bulldog', partly because of his ferocity in the debating chamber, mostly because of his impressive jowls.

Malamba was tired because he had remained at MI6 headquarters until two o'clock that morning. The interrogation – he still struggled to think of it as an interview – had taken on a dreamy, almost hallucinatory aspect. After the initial exchanges, it had become a kind of fencing match: Luard constantly thrusting at Malamba with un-expected questions about his college friends, his brother's drink problem, even what kind of car he used to drive before he acquired his own chauffeur. Luard was tenacious and unpredictable. And the space behind his eyes was cold. For his own part, Malamba had done plenty of parrying. Made a few thrusts of his own, too, but had he drawn blood? Impossible to tell.

And what about the moment when he had finally left that anonymous building with its bland stone façade and its interior of steel? Had he been released, or had he walked out of his own free will? Again, he could not be sure.

One thing he did know for certain: if he never saw Nick Luard again, it would be too soon.

For all his reputation for ferocity, the Bulldog was a welcome contrast. His voice might have been a natural sedative, but he was at least straightforward.

'You must understand,' Ploughman said, for what must have been the twelfth time, 'that yesterday's shooting puts us in a very difficult position. I must strongly recom-mend you consider abbreviating your visit.'

Mani Saiki was just as ready to repeat himself. He, at least, did it with gusto. 'Your concern for our safety is overwhelming,' he beamed, 'and I assure you we will consider your proposal very carefully. As you know we are at a very delicate stage in our business negotiations. A few days well spent in your most excellent country will lead to many years of prosperity in our own nation. If along the way we can forge the right links with the United Kingdom, then *both* our nations will prosper. It will be what you might call a "win-win" situation.'

Back and forth they went. It was another fencing match – or perhaps a prize-fight, with Saiki making a passable Ali, with his fancy footwork and lightning jabs. Only as the contest drew to a close did Malamba realise the British Bulldog was in fact no lumbering George Foreman.

'I am sure you understand our concerns,' said Ploughman, as he gathered up his papers, 'so I have taken the liberty of putting in place new transport arrangements for you both.'

'Transport arrangements?' said Malamba.

The Bulldog's jowls quivered. 'Flight tickets. For the morning of the twenty-ninth. I trust you will be able to conclude your business here within forty-eight hours. Given the precarious position of your government, I am sure you will want to press on with your tour to the US and be home sooner.'

Saiki hesitated. For a moment, Malamba thought he was going to unleash his wrath on the Foreign Secretary. Malamba was one of the few people who had ever seen Saiki lose his temper. It was a rare event, like a solar eclipse; and like that phenomenon, it made people stop in the streets and wonder why everything was going dark.

Instead, Saiki broadened his smile. 'Forty-eight hours? A most ample span of time, my dear Foreign Secretary. If we cannot cause our plans to reach fruition in that time then we are not worthy of the trust our people have placed in us. And now, good day to you, sir.'

The Bulldog made some gruff comment under his breath, then showed them out of the meeting room. As they left, Malamba glanced at the security man standing guard at the door. It was the same muscle-bound character who had turned up with Officer Paddon that morning. Seeing him reminded Malamba that Paddon's regular partner – the pretty brunette with the striking green eyes – had got herself shot protecting the man who was currently at his side grinning like a fool.

He wondered what would have happened had she not put herself in the way of the bullet. He, Paul Malamba, would be in line for the presidency, that was what.

Just as his mind was beginning to day-dream about the trappings of power, real power, Chief Inspector Paddon himself appeared at the end of the corridor. His mouth was set in a firm, straight line. As he marched towards them, he held Malamba's gaze.

'Good morning, gentlemen,' he said. Ignoring the SODs man, Vincent Ploughman was already halfway to the stairs. Paddon let him go. 'Would you accompany me, please? We have another room set aside on the ground floor. There's something we need to discuss.'

'Yes, yes,' said Saiki, trying to breeze past him, 'but whatever it is will have to wait. We have a lunch appointment at your Institute for Materials, Minerals and Mining, and we absolutely must not be late.'

Paddon extended an arm casually enough not to cause offence, sharply enough to make his intentions clear. 'I'm sorry, but this really can't wait. Don't worry, I'll make sure you don't miss your appointment. The Institute is only a few doors down the road – as soon as we're finished I'll escort you there personally.'

Again Saiki hesitated. Malamba held his breath and waited for the explosion, simultaneously horrified and fascinated.

Sooner or later he will lose control. Then they really will have reason to throw us out of the country.

'Very well,' said Saiki, at last. The smile had vanished from his face. 'But I am growing a little tired of being treated like an unwelcome guest.'

'If you'll just come with me, sir,' said Paddon, 'everything will be explained.'

At this, Saiki raised his eyebrows. 'Really, officer? For some reason I am finding that hard to believe.'

The room was small and must once have been plush. Now it smelled faintly of damp. The state of this old building was of little interest to Paul Malamba, however – he was more concerned by the size of the welcoming committee. There was Henry Worthington, the bureaucrat who had welcomed them on their arrival in the UK. With his big smile and small feet, he should have been a ballroom dancer, or perhaps a reader of the news. At Worthington's side was a short, senior policeman with a red face bearing precious few laughter lines.

Beside the policeman was Nick Luard.

Barely nine hours had passed since he had left Luard on the steps of the faceless building where MI6 did its inscrutable thing. The look on Luard's face now was exactly the same as it had been then.

I see right through you, it seemed to say.

Ignoring Luard's gaze, Malamba shuffled into the little room behind his president. Paddon closed the door behind him. For a few seconds they all stood in silence.

'I'm sorry to interrupt your schedule like this,' said Worthington, 'but I'm afraid something happened this morning that we feel you should know about. Before I inform you what it is, I should introduce Chief Superintendent Brian Burfield. He's in charge of Special Operations – Diplomats. Given what happened yesterday, you could say he is one of the reasons you're still alive to talk to us today, President Saiki.'

Saiki threw a nervous glance Malamba's way. Malamba's heart was running like a gazelle. What did these people know?

Worthington spoke again. 'There's no easy

way to say this, so I'll simply tell you the facts. Just after two-thirty this morning, one of our police patrols found the body of Piet Bakker on the outskirts of Green Park. I'm afraid he'd been murdered.'

'Murdered?' said Saiki. His reaction was almost a pantomime of shock: the dropped jaw, the hands clasped to his cheeks. But that was just Saiki – he gave the same performance if his shoes hadn't been shined properly. It seemed the British security people knew that, too: they were ignoring the president in favour of his minister. Malamba felt their eyes drilling into him: Worthington's, Burfield's and Luard's. Especially Luard's.

They found the body at two-thirty, he thought. *Just when I was arriving back at the hotel. And they know it.*

'As yet,' Worthington went on, addressing Saiki, 'we have not informed the press about this regrettable incident. We thought it best to inform you, however, given your relationship with Mr Bakker and the sensitive nature of your visit. Also, I must tell you that we may wish to interview both you and Mr Malamba with regard to the murder.'

Saiki's eyes widened. 'Surely you do not think we had anything to do with it?'

Burfield stepped forward. 'Nobody's suggesting that, President Saiki. But you might be able to help us find the killer. I'm sure you want that as much as we do.'

'Well, of course. These people must be found.' Saiki turned to Malamba. 'Do you not agree, Paul?'

'Of course,' said Malamba. His lips felt numb. Could Luard's X-ray eyes see through his chest to his racing heart? Of course they could. He wanted to run. All the way back to Africa. He had never felt so far from home.

And yet ... this was good news. *Bakker dead!* That meant the nationalisation plans would go ahead unopposed. Removing Bakker was like removing a mountain range. Now he could build his highway right out to the horizon, with nothing standing in his way.

His mind was racing to match his heart-beat. *Speed is the key.* Could he set up the cash flow quickly enough to take advantage of this unexpected boon? If so, he could get far more out of this visit to the UK than he had ever imagined. Instead of returning to the Republic of Limpopo with an attaché case full of mere outline proposals, there was a good chance he would be carrying, if not actual contracts, then certainly signed letters-of-intent. Actual agreements with British suppliers to provide the Republic with the technology it needed to bring its mines into the twenty-first century. When he stepped off the plane, the Limpopo business community would be showering him with rose petals.

Luckily, the people he needed to consult to set all this up would be attending today's lunch at the Institute for Materials, Minerals and Mining. It would be the perfect opportunity to arrange formal meetings with them. With one man in particular, in fact. Never mind the short notice – they would practically bite his hand off. Malamba almost smiled at the thought, then stopped himself. He had just had bad news. It would not do to look too cheerful.

Saiki was asking about Bakker's death. Burfield explained that the body had been found with its throat cut. Malamba shivered at the image this conjured up; but there was something thrilling about it all the same. It was no more than the bastard deserved.

'It is a remarkable coincidence,' said Saiki, addressing the little room as if it were a chamber full of potential voters, 'that this crime should have been committed at this precise moment in time. Think of it: Piet

Bakker dies just as we were about to reveal to him our plans to nationalise all his Limpopo mining interests. It is what you might call *poetic*. We will, of course, help you with your enquiries, but for now you will forgive me if I turn my attention to the immediate effect this news has on our business dealings here in your country.' He turned to Malamba. 'Sad as I am, Paul, to hear of this dreadful atrocity, I am pleased that my excellent Minister for Minerals will now be able to progress his plans in a forward direction without Bakker Diamonds and Minerals standing in the way.'

Grasping Malamba's head in his hands, Saiki planted a kiss on his brow. Then he beamed at his astonished audience. 'If you will excuse us, gentleman, we have a new national economy to construct.'

Saiki was back on form. Like a ball of lightning, he crackled round the room, shaking hands with Worthington and the others. Meanwhile, Malamba stood dumbfounded. In a single breath, his president had just confirmed to the British government, police and secret service that he, Malamba, had the perfect motive for killing Bakker.

Apparently unaware of what he had done,

227

Saiki grabbed Malamba's arm and swept him out of the room. As they departed, Malamba could still feel those eyes on the back of his neck, Luard's most of all.

As he had promised, Charlie Paddon accompanied them on the short walk down the block to the Institute. The sky was bright and clear after the previous day's storm. Malamba turned his face up to the sun, enjoying its heat. He missed the African horizon. Here in London, the sky was cramped by the buildings.

'How is your colleague, officer?' asked Saiki, when they reached the Institute. 'I have already expressed my gratitude for her bravery by way of a large bouquet of flowers and a small card, but I would be most grateful if you could pass on my salutations when you see her.'

'She's doing fine, thank you,' said Paddon. 'She should be out of hospital today.'

'Do you know her well enough to visit her at home? I think perhaps you do.'

'Uh, yes.'

'So, when you see her, you will tell her what I have said?'

'Of course, President Saiki.'

Paddon waited as they went through the door, then turned away. Malamba watched him cross the road and get into the red BMW parked on the opposite kerb. And there he would wait while they ate lunch and shook hands and struck their deals.

He wondered what was going through the SODs man's mind. Who was he really there to protect? The two visitors from the Republic of Limpopo? Or was it they who were the threat?

Perhaps he is there not to protect us at all, but to stop us making trouble. It is not the safety of diplomats that concerns him, but the safety of his country.

It was a cynical thought, and one that sat uncomfortably with him. The door closed, obscuring his view of the street. Then someone was seizing and pumping his hand. He turned to see a familiar face.

'Good to see you again, Malamba!' the man cried. 'Come on through – the buffet's well and truly open. This time I think we can do a bit better than warm London Porter in a cracked glass!'

18

June 27th

16:19

Redbreast Avenue, Brentford

Danni the nanny was compact, gorgeous, blonde and Australian, and Charlie often wondered why Alex had ever let her in the house.

'Aren't you worried Lawrie will make a play for her?' he'd said, after meeting Danni for the first time.

'What you really mean,' Alex replied, with a mischievous smile, 'is *you'd* like to make a play for her.' This had been during Alex's matchmaking phase. She was, as ever, as subtle as an airstrike.

'The thought hadn't entered my head.'

'Liar. Anyway, Lawrie would never go with anyone who makes every sentence sound like a question.'

'Hey!' said Danni emerging from the

kitchen. 'Not everybody in Australia talks like that you know.' Her intonation lifted towards the end of her sentence.

'No, dear. But you do.'

'Is this that hunky partner you keep telling me about?' Danni made a show of looking Charlie up and down. 'See you around, big fella.'

She danced out into the garden with a basket of washing in her arms.

'You could do worse,' said Alex, watching Charlie's expression. 'You haven't had a girlfriend since you broke up with Kathy. It's not natural.'

'We were together six years, Alex.'

'Doesn't mean it takes six years to get over it. Why don't you ask her out?'

'She's not my type.'

Out in the garden, Danni was reaching up to hang the clothes and exposing a remarkable amount of trim midriff in the process. 'Charlie, you've got to be kidding.'

Charlie remembered that exchange now as Danni opened the door to Alex's Brentford semi. It being June, there was even more stomach on display than usual. And it was seriously tanned. Hiding behind a pair of equally bronzed legs was a two year-old boy with the same sandy hair as his father.

'Hi, big fella,' Danni said. 'Alex said you'd be calling. Why don't you come in?'

'Thanks, Danni,' he said. He tried to keep his eyes off her belly button – which now sported a piercing in the shape of a dolphin – and reminded himself that, gorgeous as she was, the every-sentence-is-a-question thing really would drive you crazy.

The house was filled with summer light and smelled of fresh flowers. The stained-glass panel on the front door splashed streams of colour on the wooden floor of the hall. A straight line led through hall and kitchen and out through the back door to the garden, where a plastic sandpit basked in the sun.

'Hi, Fraser,' Charlie said. 'You've grown. How old are you now? Ten?'

Fraser giggled. Then he remembered to be bashful and his mouth snapped shut.

'I like your T-shirt. It looks like Liquorice Allsorts.'

That was enough for Fraser. He released his grip on Danni's legs and barrelled down to the other end of the hall, where he had about thirty Matchbox cars lined up in some kind of procession. The sandpit was clearly inferior entertainment. Dropping to his tummy, he started inching the cars forwards, one at a time. Within seconds, he was utterly absorbed.

Charlie imagined the day when toy cars wouldn't be enough and Fraser started asking for a ride in the red BMW. That would be fun – if he could get the idea past Alex. He could hear her now, fussing about booster seats and gender stereotyping and the effects of G-forces on the infant brain. Of course, if Alex went to Dubai, the problem would never arise

'He's so pleased his daddy's come home,' said Danni. 'Alex says as long as he's here they should hang out as much as they can. She wants them to spend the day together tomorrow, if she can tear Lawrie away from his work. It's tough on the nipper with his daddy being in Scotland, you know?'

'Yes,' said Charlie. 'I can imagine.'

'How's your girl?'

'Girl? Oh, you mean Jackie. She's not really my girl.'

'You taking her to the movies again? You should, you know? Only, take my advice: pick one that doesn't have explosions.'

When did my private life get to be so public? Maybe someone was putting it on a website somewhere.

The study door was closed. As they passed it, Charlie heard two men talking. One of them was Lawrie. He lowered his voice and asked:

'How is she, Danni? Is she okay?'

Danni's teeth shone through her tan. 'She's doing great. Looks a bit like shit, to be honest, but you should have seen her face when she saw Fraser again. She's better off out of that hospital, that's for sure. Those places are just so depressing. You want some coffee? I was just going to make a pot.'

'Sure, thanks, that would be great.'

'Cool – she's in the back room. Go on through.'

Alex was stretched out on the squashy sofa under the window. Threadbare on the arms, the sofa looked like it had seen better days; so did Alex. But when she saw Charlie her face filled with colour and the dark circles under her eyes went pink.

'Hey, partner,' she said. The words came out in a croak. She coughed and took a swig from a bottle of water balanced on the arm of the sofa. Beside the bottle was a huge bunch of flowers.

'Are you all right?' said Charlie, perching on the arm of the adjacent chair. 'You don't sound good.'

'Thanks. I'm just tired, really. Either that or I picked up some superbug in the hospital that even now is eating me up from the inside out.'

She tried to sit up, and failed, pulling a face. 'Whoa,' said Charlie. 'Don't try and move on my account. I'm the one who put you there after all.'

Alex stared at him. 'What the hell are you talking about?'

Charlie swallowed. He hated seeing her like this. He wanted her back in action. 'I mean, I took my eye off the ball. I was too busy with Bakker to notice...'

'Don't be silly.'

'...to notice what was going on. I kept replaying it my head last night. If I'd just been quicker up the steps...'

She put down the water bottle and took his hand. 'Look, we went through all this. It's the risk we take every time we put on the uniform. You know that. Besides, it all balances out. Next time it's your turn to get shot.'

'Thanks, partner.'

'Don't mention it.'

The sound of laughter filtered through from the study. With a jerk, Charlie pulled his hand away.

'I'm sorry,' he said. 'If it's an awkward time...'

Alex brushed her hair back out of her eyes.

'No, it's all right. When Bob realised Lawrie was down here he arranged to come over. Bob was in London anyway, cracking the whip or something, so it made sense to get him round so we could all talk about the move to Dubai together.'

'And you're all right with that? Entertaining the Chief Executive of Lochavon Industries when you're on your sick bed?'

She looked away. 'I know you don't like the idea of me going abroad, Charlie.'

Danni interrupted with the coffee. Charlie's gaze lingered on her as she put down the tray and left the room. Too late, he realised Alex was watching him.

'How's Jackie?' she said.

'Don't you start.'

Alex took another mouthful of water. Charlie stared out of the window. The murmur of voices continued to filter through from the study. Out in the hall, Fraser made the cars go *vroom*.

'Why don't you...?' began Alex at the same time as Charlie said, 'I thought I'd...' They both laughed. The tension broken, Alex said, 'Tell me what's been going on today. I feel like I'm missing out on something big.'

'Well, I guess I should start with Piet Bakker.'

'They don't come much bigger. Have we found him?'

'Yes. At least, we found his body.'

'His *body?* He's dead?'

'Murdered.'

'Holy shit.'

She inched herself into a sitting position. The crease in her brow told Charlie she was either in pain or thinking very hard. Probably both.

'Gory details,' she demanded. 'Right now.'

He told her everything they knew. When she asked about suspects, he told her how Nick Luard had kept Malamba at MI6 until the wee hours.

'Do you think he did it?' said Alex.

Charlie frowned. 'The motive's certainly there. Luard thinks he did – it's written all over his face. But ... I don't know. I don't think it's as simple as that.'

'But you think he might be involved? An accessory?'

'I don't know. I keep thinking about that meeting he had in the pub. I wish I knew who that man was. Something's going on. I just can't work out what.'

'You know your trouble where Malamba's concerned?'

'What?'

'You like the guy.' She wriggled on the sofa, trying to get comfortable. 'You know, the worst thing is I can't stretch without hurting. My body feels like it needs a good going over, you know what I mean?'

'That's quite a bunch of flowers,' said Charlie, standing up. 'Are they from Saiki?'

'No – Brian. Saiki had some sent to the hospital though. Wasn't that sweet?'

'Thoughtful.'

'Chocolates are nicer.'

Charlie couldn't hear the voices in the study any more. It was time to leave. They wouldn't want him around while they all discussed Lawrie's transfer. It wasn't something he wanted to hear about anyway.

'I should be going,' he said.

'You didn't drink your coffee.'

Alex looked so forlorn he relented and poured himself a cup. It was lukewarm but he tossed it back all the same. 'There,' he said. 'Now, I really must go.'

There was a muffled click as the study door opened. Footsteps echoed in the hall. Seconds later, the door to the living-room swung open and Lawrie walked in. His eyes were shining with excitement.

'Hey, Charlie, good to see you. Thanks for keeping the old girl company while we've been planning global domination. Hey, honey, have we got some ideas or what? I tell you, a few months from now, you won't be lying in that old wreck of a sofa – you'll be sitting by the pool drinking ... well, probably tonic water if we're honest ... you know what these countries are like for alcohol...'

'It's only Dubai, Lawrie...'

'...but anyway, you'll be by the pool soaking up the sun and we'll be living the life of Riley!'

His exuberance was so boyish, so unaffected, Charlie couldn't help but smile. Out in the hall, Fraser was doing his best to remove the varnish from the wooden floor by recreating a motorway pile-up. In the doorway, half-hidden by Lawrie, a tall man was standing, waiting to be introduced.

'Darling,' said Alex, 'it's not polite to hog the limelight when your boss is standing right behind you.'

Bustling out of the way, Lawrie allowed the man to enter the room. 'Charlie!' he cried. 'You haven't met Bob, have you? Bob – this is Chief Inspector Charlie Paddon, my wife's partner-in-crime, if you'll forgive the expression. And Charlie, this is Bob Pettifer, the man who pays my mortgage.'

Charlie painted a smile on his face and

raised a hand made of lead. 'Hello, Bob,' he said, forcing the words to come out naturally. 'I've heard a lot about you.'

In the corner of his vision he could see Alex eyeing him with a faintly quizzical expression. Flat out on the sofa she might have been, but she was still as attuned as ever to Charlie's thoughts. Whatever it was she saw in his reaction, Lawrie had missed it completely. He hoped Bob Pettifer had missed it, too.

'Always a pleasure to meet an officer of the law,' boomed Pettifer, seizing Charlie's hand and pumping it vigorously. The action sent a ripple of movement through his wavy grey hair, like an ocean swell. 'Were you on your way out?'

'Yes,' said Charlie. 'I was just leaving.' He turned to Alex. 'I might call you later. With a status report.'

'I'll be here,' she replied. Their eyes locked briefly, then he turned away.

'Never off duty, eh?' laughed Pettifer, as Charlie stepped out into the hall.

'Not very often,' he replied. 'Nice to meet you, Bob.'

From the corner there was a tremendous smash as Fraser dropped one handful of cars on top of another.

'Crash!' he shouted, his voice echoing down the hall.

Charlie let himself out. As he shut the door behind him, he closed his eyes. The image of Bob Pettifer's face lingered. It was the first time they'd been introduced, but he'd seen the man with the rock-and-roll hair before, drinking London Porter in a little Mayfair pub called Ye Grapes, with the Republic of Limpopo Minister for Minerals, Paul Malamba.

19

June 27th

17:00

SODs Headquarters, New Scotland Yard

It didn't take long for the news of Bakker's death to break. Henry heard a report on BBC Radio Four's five o'clock bulletin, and wondered where they'd picked up the story. Had it come from his department? The notion offended him. It wasn't that he disapproved of government leaks – it was just that when there were leaks to be made he'd rather he was the one tweaking the taps.

Brian Burfield called while he was listening to the news. 'Can you come over?' he said, as terse as ever.

'To Scotland Yard?' Henry replied. 'Now? Really, Brian, do you think I can just rearrange my day at the drop of a hat? What's it about? Is it important?'

'Could be. It's about the Africans.'

'Would you care to share any details with me?'

'Not over the phone. Can you be here in twenty minutes?'

Henry muttered some nonsense about schedules and cancelling appointments. He even emptied out his in-tray and shuffled the papers near the phone. But the truth was he'd done most of what he needed to today and the clatter of the pneumatic drills was turning his teeth to tinfoil.

'I'll try and get away before six,' he said, at last, and put the phone down.

As he made the short walk from Whitehall to New Scotland Yard, it occurred to him that this was the first time he'd left work at something like a sensible hour in ... how long? The heat of the day had yet to depart and the sky looked like something out of a Wedgewood kiln. When he stopped to listen he fancied he could hear a nightingale.

Was he what people called a workaholic? He wasn't sure he knew the meaning of the word. His sister told him he was, but she said the same about her husband. 'You and Jack,' she would say, 'you're more alike than you care to admit.' But Mary had always been one to fuss. What was her weekly invitation to Sunday lunch if not a clumsy attempt to mother him?

Henry remembered reading somewhere that most Englishmen measured success in terms of career and marriage. Well, he'd never married, so was it any wonder he was committed to the job? Besides, what else was there? If he lived in Africa maybe he'd be judged on how many cattle he owned, but this was Whitehall and there were precious few dairy herds in sight.

Anyway, there is more to my life than work. I was thinking about joining the archery club again, and there's always something on at the theatre. And it's about time I redecorated the flat.

When he thought about it, there really was an awful lot to be getting on with. And very little time left to do it all: in another five years he'd be in line for the early retirement he'd always promised himself. Always assuming he'd made it onto Her Majesty's Honours List by then.

Burfield was waiting with his usual mug of builder's tea. Henry considered asking him for the recipe: he'd need a decent paint-stripper when he started on the flat.

'Well, here I am,' he announced, throwing his silk scarf on the back of the chair.

'Before six, as promised. This had better be good, Brian.'

Compared to Henry's office, Burfield's was tiny. Instead of the marble fireplace there was a set of steel shelves bending under the weight of countless legal tomes and policy folders. Where Henry's desk was gleaming walnut, Burfield sat behind gloomy teak. And his laptop looked like it was steam-powered.

'I need a favour,' said Burfield, when Henry had sat down.

'A favour? You called me all this way for a *favour*?'

'Come on, Henry. It's on your way home.'

'That's hardly the point. Do you realise I've abandoned a mountain of paperwork the size of Alaska just to...'

'How big?'

'What?'

'The paperwork. Size of a mountain, or size of Alaska? Can't be both.'

Henry gritted his teeth. 'Just tell me what you want.'

'Chap called Robert Pettifer. I've got people checking him out. He's a big cheese but he's proving elusive. You're a university man – I thought you might be able to dig a bit deeper. Pull a few strings.'

'What are you talking about?' *He's as bad as Luard!*

'Humour me. I need to know if Pettifer's got any connections with York University. Late seventies, early eighties.'

And you call yourself a policeman? 'Haven't you ever heard of the internet?'

Circling the desk, Henry shunted Burfield's chair aside and opened the web browser on his laptop. Odd – the thought of Brian using a computer seemed like something of an evolutionary step. He tried to ignore the mouse mat, which revealed a picture of a leering British Bulldog. Crumbs were visible in the cracks of the keyboard.

He went straight to Friends Reunited and logged on. He'd registered as a user some years before, but had only ever used the site to read the pages set up by people he'd known at boarding school or Cambridge. Jack had told him such behaviour had a name: *lurking.*

Maybe that's why Luard and Burfield both keep asking me to play at spies.

The York University pages threw up several Pettifers but nobody with the first name of Robert or Bob. He went to Google and typed 'Robert Pettifer York University' into the search box. There were thousands of results listed, but the only direct match was a Professor of French who'd worked there in the fifties. 'We could cast the net wider,' said Henry, 'but it really depends on what you mean by "connections". Perhaps this Pettifer chap didn't have anything to do with the university. Forgive me, Brian, but isn't this what you have detectives for?'

Brian swallowed his tea and looked mournful. 'We are looking, Henry. My guess is we're drawing a blank because that's all there is to be drawn.'

Henry sat back down in his chair, pulled it up to the desk.

'Right,' he said. 'You're going to tell me exactly what you're talking about right now. Start with this Bob Pettifer. Who is he, and why are you so interested in him?'

So Burfield told him. He began by explaining how, two nights previously, Charlie Paddon had followed Paul Malamba to a pub in Mayfair. 'Charlie was officially off-duty,' Burfield said, 'but it was right after you and I had that talk. When you told us to back off.'

'I don't recall using those words, Brian.'

'Whatever you said, that's what you meant. Lucky for us, Paddon's got more about him than most. Anyway, Malamba goes to the pub and meets a bloke Charlie doesn't recognise. They talk. They drink beer. It all looks a bit cloak and dagger, but Charlie can't pin anything down. Then, this afternoon, Charlie's visiting Alex Chappell at home and guess who turns up? Malamba's friend. Turns out his name's Bob Pettifer and he runs Lochavon Industries. Now, Lochavon's built on oil and coal but Pettifer's taking them deeper and deeper into Silicon Valley territory. Seems they've got the best technology in the world when it comes to getting stuff out of the ground. Stuff like oil and coal. Also stuff like diamonds and cobalt.'

'Where did you get all this information?'

Burfield grinned. 'I have detectives, remember?'

'Where does Sergeant Chappell fit into all this? Why was Pettifer there?'

'Alex's husband works for Pettifer. Pure coincidence. Lucky for us though.'

Henry shook his head, trying to sort through this new information. 'So you think this Pettifer is connected with Malamba somehow? Beyond just meeting him in a pub, I mean.'

'It's possible. It might be perfectly innocent. Maybe they were talking rocks. I'm just gathering what information I can. You think you can help?'

Henry stood, took his scarf from the chair and tossed it over his shoulder. His head felt too full. 'Let me think about it,' he said. 'I'll see what I can come up with.'

He left Burfield tapping on his keyboard. The man was the only one-finger typist he'd ever met. But then, it had taken a while for the World Wide Web to reach Yorkshire – the man had a lot of catching up to do.

For the second time in as many days, Henry made for The Mall. It was a small diversion, but a useful one. His thoughts were darting one way and another; he needed to get them lined up. The Mall, straight as an arrow, would do that for him.

Connections. It's all about connections.

The so-called 'British connection'. Ever since Jack had hinted at it in that wretched article in *The Times*, they'd been talking about it, skirting round it, never really getting to the bottom of it. Now, perhaps they were getting close to identifying the players in that grubby little game that had siphoned government money out of the Republic of Limpopo, through British hands and back into the coffers of Bakker Diamonds and Minerals.

Malamba. Bakker. Pettifer.

What if Luard was right, and Malamba really was the villain of the piece? What if Malamba hadn't only worked for Bakker, but had been in on all his dodgy deals to boot? Malamba knew Britain well – had been to university here, for goodness' sake. He'd have had plenty of opportunity to make friends with influential industrialists. Industrialists like Bob Pettifer, for instance.

Was that it? Was Pettifer the British connection? Henry rolled the thought round, tasted it. It was possible.

Bakker pays President Kissonga a small fortune as a bribe for the privilege of running his mines. Kissonga can't launder all the money, so some of it disappears out of the Republic of Limpopo and ends up in Britain – in Scotland, actually, where a pair of friendly hands moves it through the books of several mining operations – operations like Lochavon Industries, for instance. More likely, through companies that exist only on paper. Eventually the money gets back to the Republic of Limpopo in the form of investment in ... you guessed it, Bakker Diamonds and Minerals. Also in about a hundred little businesses in which Kissonga's the major shareholder. Bakker's showing a huge profit anyway, because he's exploiting his workforce and cutting his costs to the bone, which means he can pay Kissonga ever bigger bribes. Round and round it goes. While the people of the Republic of Limpopo are struggling to make ends meet, Bakker and Kissonga are living – almost literally – off the fat of the land.

A set-up like that might have benefited from a bright, articulate man with a passion for the British way of life. Someone well-placed to ... *facilitate*. Someone like Paul Malamba.

Henry had reached the gates of Buckingham Palace. He stood for a moment, feeling infinitely superior to the tourists bunched at intervals along the iron railing. This was his realm, his world. In a week, maybe two, they would return to their own countries and he would remain here, at the heart of it all.

Turning south, he headed for home.

His theory raised an interesting possibility: that Jack McClintock's mysterious informant was none other than Paul Malamba himself. The more he thought about it, the more it made sense. Malamba, like the others, must have profited from the 'Bakker-hander' operation. Up until recently it would have been a four-way split: Kissonga, Bakker, Malamba, Pettifer. As soon as Kissonga was ousted, it became a three-way

251

split. That was when Malamba got greedy. He had a wife and three kids to support, after all. And a growing taste for power. In his new position as Minister for Minerals, he saw an opportunity to write Bakker out of the script. That was what the nationalisation was all about. That much at least had been clear from the start. It was only now that the real reasons behind it were becoming clear.

With Bakker down, that left Malamba and Pettifer. By leaking information to the British press, Malamba could effectively take Pettifer out of the game too. He hadn't actually given Pettifer's name to Jack yet, but it was only a matter of time.

Malamba murdered Bakker!

Despite the warmth of the evening, this final realisation sent a chill through Henry's bones. There was a murderer loose in London. Worse than that, the signature at the bottom of the documents authorising the diplomatic visit, admitting the murderer to the country in the first place, was that of Henry Edward Worthington.

No matter. Documents could be filed. Henry had a number of very deep drawers at his disposal. First things first though: Malamba had to go down.

Henry's flat was just round the corner

from Westminster Cathedral. Usually, Henry paused beneath the great Catholic façade – not to admire it but to try and work out why he found it so hideous. This evening he walked straight past without giving it a second glance.

Once inside his flat, he clicked on the kettle and dropped three spoons of jasmine tea in his favourite Spode pot. While the water boiled, he picked up the phone and dialled Jack's direct line at *The Times*. It was nearly seven o'clock, but it didn't even occur to him Jack wouldn't be at his desk.

Jack picked up on the third ring, proving Mary's theory that he was at least as wedded to his career as Henry.

'Jack – it's Henry.'

'Hello, old man. Still at the office?'

'Actually, no. I've just come from Scotland Yard.'

'Oh yes. Something up? Is it that juicy murder that got picked up this afternoon? Stroke of luck, really. I know the news already broke on the agencies but wait 'til you see our front page tomorrow. One of our freelancers has, um, acquired some CCTV footage from near the Piccadilly lights. He was researching those high-class hookers for which Mayfair is so rightly famous, but while he was going through this morning's footage he found what looked like an entire division of the Met cleaning up a crime scene on the edge of Green Park. Next thing we've got tentative confirmation from the boys in blue and a press conference, well, any minute now. Care to comment, Henry? Strictly off-the-record, of course.'

Henry suppressed a groan. He might have known Jack would be at the front of the pack of hounds. 'That isn't why I called,' he said. 'I called because I know who's been feeding you information about Piet Bakker's criminal activities.' Silence on the line. That had shut him up. Henry went on. 'It was Paul Malamba, wasn't it?'

To his astonishment, Jack burst out laughing. While Henry waited for him to explain himself, the kettle boiled and switched itself off. He filled the pot, savouring the sweet smell of jasmine as it filled the kitchen.

'Oh, Henry,' Jack spluttered, 'you do come out with some corkers.'

'I don't know what you mean,' said Henry. Angry now, he slammed the lid on the pot and dropped the cosy over the top.

'No. I don't suppose you do. Well, I'll put you out of your misery. Now that bastard Bakker's dead I can talk freely again. No need to worry about lawsuits now. Or having my kneecaps broken. I don't mind telling you, it's a weight off my mind. I was jumping at every shadow, Henry. Mary was going up the wall. Still, at least the boys are safe now. If that bastard had ever so much as...'

'Jack.'

'What?'

'Just tell what's so fucking funny.'

'Oh, that. The informant. It wasn't Malamba telling me all about dodgy deals down the Limpopo mines. Whatever gave you that idea? It was Bakker.'

20

June 27th

23:19

Morpeth Terrace, London

Charlie followed Brian up the stairs to Henry Worthington's flat. Charlie half-expected to find him in his dressing-gown and slippers, but when Henry answered the door he was still dressed as if for the office.

'Would you like some tea?' Henry asked as they went through to the living-room. 'I'm sorry the place is looking a bit shabby. I'm thinking of decorating.'

Charlie wondered what he was talking about: the flat looked like something out of *House & Garden*. Charlie declined the offer of tea. Brian, however, said yes, with some enthusiasm. When Henry served up a delicate china cup full of his best jasmine, the Chief Superintendent's face was a picture.

Nick Luard was already there, reclining in

a chintzy wing-back chair as if he owned the place. He was holding a glass of port. Brian's private thoughts appeared in red neon on his forehead: *Why wasn't I offered that?* Charlie positioned himself strategically between the two antagonists, just in case.

'I thought it best we all get together,' said Henry, pacing up and down the long room. 'Things are moving fast and if we don't get on top of them ... well, who knows what might happen next?'

'Where d'you want to start?' said Brian.

Luard leaned forward in his chair. 'Why don't you start with Jack McClintock, Henry?'

'Good idea. Brian, Charlie – before you arrived I was filling Nick in on the background to these news articles *The Times* has been pumping out.'

'The ones about how Bakker's been ripping off the people of the Republic for the last thirty years?' said Charlie.

'They're the ones. Well, it turns out the person who's been giving Jack the scoop on all that is none other than Piet Bakker himself.'

Charlie tried that one on for size. Whichever way he turned it, he couldn't get it to fit. 'I don't get it,' he said.

Warming to his role, Henry continued. 'As soon as Kissonga lost power, Bakker knew his position was shaky. So he set about consolidating it.'

'And how did stitching himself up help with that?'

'Think about it. With Kissonga gone, Bakker had three choices. One: bury his head and carry on as if nothing had happened, which would ultimately mean submitting to whatever indignities the new regime forced upon him, not least the nationalisation of his entire Republic of Limpopo operation. Two: cut and run. But there was his pride to consider.'

'And the third option?' said Brian, stirring his tea with a look of revulsion.

'Bakker must have had some hint of what would happen once Kissonga was ousted – that his days were numbered. He was trying to shore up his claims to power by blackmailing his UK contacts.

'How?' asked Charlie. He glanced at the antique clock on the bookcase. This was all very interesting but they hadn't come here to talk about a dead man. There was a lot still at stake, and wasting time now might mean another corpse on their hands. Still, he wanted to know.

'By threatening to expose the rotten core,' said Henry. 'The article was a risk – a controlled risk. Revealing the whiff of something bad, but short of naming names. It was basically a message to Pettifer: "My way or the highway".'

'Bakker was playing politics,' said Charlie.

'And it looks like he was the one who got played,' said Brian. 'Malamba and Lochavon decided to take the wagging tongue out of the picture.'

'Which is why,' said Nick Luard, placing his port on the varnished coffee table, 'we need the surveillance operation.'

'Well, Nick, you know how I feel about that,' began Henry, hastily tossing Luard a coaster. Brian stopped him by raising his hand.

'Hold it,' he growled. 'What surveillance operation?'

Charlie and Brian listened while Luard told them about a telephone conversation Malamba had made two hours previously. The call had been made from a public telephone in the lobby of the Charles Darwin Hotel to the London office of Lochavon Industries.

'The conversation lasted a little over a minute,' Luard said, 'during which time Malamba arranged a private meeting between himself and Bob Pettifer in the Lochavon Chequer Room at Canary Wharf. The meeting's booked for nine o'clock tomorrow morning.'

'You've tapped the hotel phones?' said Brian. Luard delivered his best MI6 smirk to the room at large. 'Let me guess – now you want to bug the meeting?'

'It's the logical thing to do,' said Luard.

'Don't worry, Brian,' put in Henry. 'That's not going to happen.'

Charlie spoke up. 'Actually,' he said, 'I have to agree with Nick. Whatever's said in that meeting, it's vital we know what it is.'

Very slowly, Brian turned his head. Just as slowly, he put his cup and saucer down on the table next to Nick Luard's half-empty glass of port. Henry went in search of another coaster. 'Chief Inspector Paddon,' he said. 'Do you have any idea what you're saying?'

Charlie felt his back stiffen. 'All I'm saying, sir, is we need to know what's going on. I know it's not exactly standard police procedure...'

'Too bloody right!'

'...but it's the only way.'

'I think you should listen to your superior

officer,' said Henry. 'If it came out we'd mounted an unauthorised surveillance operation on a visiting foreign minister, not to mention the private offices of a successful corporation, it'd be all our necks on the chopping block. Not to mention all our faces lined up under Jack McClintock's next headline.'

'But there's no time,' said Charlie. How could he convince them? Much as it grieved him to side with the slimy Luard, he really couldn't see a better way of handling this. Put Malamba and Pettifer in the same room, and you'd get all the answers you needed. But they had to act fast: the meeting was barely nine hours away. 'If we're going to do it, we've got to do it now.'

'I'm not about to break the rules,' said Brian.

'And I'm not prepared to risk my career,' said Henry. 'All our careers,' he added hastily.

Charlie looked to Nick Luard for help. But Luard, curiously, just sat in his chair looking like the Cheshire cat.

'Look, Mr Worthington,' said Charlie. 'Think about what might happen if we *don't* put a glass to the wall on this one. Let's assume Malamba and Pettifer are preparing to cook up some kind of deal in there. We've got one man dead and an officer who's lucky to be alive. Who knows what else they might be planning? Or what if you're right, and Malamba really *is* the murderer? Following your logic, Pettifer's likely to be his next victim. We need to stop this now, before anyone else gets hurt. You can be sure of one thing, Henry – if the next bullet finds President Saiki then the headlines really *will* be worth reading.'

Henry's sudden pallor told Charlie he'd struck a chord. Which left Brian.

'And as far as the rulebook goes,' he said, giving his boss a sideways glance, 'we're in a closed room in the middle of the night in the presence of the head of MI6. Do we really need any more authority than that?'

Brian threw up his hands. 'Henry?' he said. 'Where's the bog? I need to puke.'

Luard seemed happy that Charlie had done his arguing for him. By the time Brian returned he'd gathered them round Henry's small dining table.

'This is now a campaign meeting,' he said. 'Thank you, Charlie, for laying out our options so clearly.'

For doing your dirty work, you mean,

thought Charlie.

'If we're going to do this,' said Brian, plonking himself down on one of the dining chairs, 'we'll need someone on the inside.'

'Yes, Brian,' said Luard, 'I was coming to that. Clearly we can't just waltz into the Lochavon Industry offices in the middle of the night without some kind of cover story. Any ideas?'

The four men exchanged glances. 'Isn't it obvious?' said Henry. 'Sergeant Chappell's husband. What's his name? Laurence?'

'Lawrie,' said Charlie, quietly.

'Exactly. It's perfect. He works there – I'm sure he can get us in and out with the minimum of fuss.'

And when we're all caught with our pants down, thought Charlie, *Lawrie gets caught, too. Alex would never forgive me if I lost Lawrie his career.*

'That won't work,' he said. The others stared at him. 'Lawrie works in Aberdeen. He's only down here because Alex got shot. The staff at Canary Wharf won't know him.'

'He'll have an ID card,' said Luard.

Charlie shook his head. 'We need someone they know by sight. Someone with some authority. We might need access codes, that sort of thing.'

Brian was nodding. 'Charlie's right. Lawrie's a non-starter.' The flicker in his eyes told Charlie they were on the same page: *let's keep the Chappells out of this.*

'Then who do you suggest'?' said Henry, throwing his hands up in frustration.

Charlie reached into the back of his mind. There was something there, like a word on the end of your tongue. Something to do with Dubai? Or was it China? Why China, for heaven's sake? Not Lawrie but Alex. Somebody Alex had met once – no, someone she *knew.*

'Chen!' he blurted. Everyone turned towards him. 'Mary Chen. She runs the Lochavon HR department down here in London. Alex knows her, says she's one of the good guys. She even tried to ... never mind.'

He looked from Nick to Henry to Brian. Slowly, Nick began to nod.

'All right – we might be getting somewhere,' he said. 'HR Director – I like the sound of that. When the lady who hires and fires turns up after dark, you don't ask questions. In fact, you probably keep your head down and look the other way. Charlie – I think you've cracked it.'

'Now we just need to find her,' said Henry.

'I doubt she's sitting behind her desk waiting for us to call.'

Charlie had pulled out his notebook and was leafing through it. What were the chances he'd written the number in there? Pretty poor. 'I guess we should start with directory enquiries,' he said, when he drew a blank. Then, as he flipped the book shut, a scrappy piece of paper dropped out. It must have been bunched into the spine. Written on it in Alex's handwriting were three mobile numbers. Beside each number was a name: *Dezzy, Mary, Gail.*

'Here it is,' he said, holding up the paper. More quizzical looks from his colleagues round the table.

'I won't ask,' said Brian, 'why Lochavon's HR Director figures on a list of numbers that looks like it belongs in a public phone box.'

'It's a long story,' said Charlie.

Henry handed him the phone. Hoping it was the right Mary, he dialled the number. It was now nearly midnight. Would she pick up?

'Mary Chen,' said a brisk, businesslike voice. She sounded more awake than anyone had a right to at this time of night.

'Miss Chen, this is Chief Inspector Paddon of Special Operations, Diplomats. I'm sorry to call you so late, but...'

'Charlie Paddon? Alex's Charlie?'

'Uh, yes, that's me.'

'Is Alex all right? I mean, I saw the news and everything. Oh God! She's not...?'

'Alex is fine. It could have been a lot worse.'

'Oh, that's a relief. Please, tell her I'm thinking about her. Well, this is a turn-up. Charlie Paddon ... Alex said you might call but that was over a year ago. You've left it pretty late. And I don't just mean the time of day.' She gave a warm chuckle that sent all the briskness packing. Charlie switched hands and turned away to hide the slight flush in his cheeks.

'I'm actually calling on official business, Miss Chen. There's something we need you to do for us.'

21

June 28th

00:41

Lochavon Industries, Canary Wharf

Charlie gazed across the moonlit water, imagining it full of tall ships and red-sailed barges. The industrial River Thames – it was hard to picture now. Skyscrapers and renovated wharves crowded the quay. The Lochavon office building was modest compared to some of its neighbours. Nevertheless, it oozed style. A place of industry, to be sure, although it felt like a long way from the coal face.

As far as this business is concerned, he thought, *the coal face is several thousand miles away in a little African country called the Republic of Limpopo.*

It might have been about diamonds and cobalt. It might have been about personal vendettas and national pride. But in the end, weren't all the players just trying to strike gold?

A silver Lexus purred up the drive. Charlie left his two companions under the ornamental trees and went over to open the door. A small woman with short black hair took his hand and allowed him to help her out.

'Thanks for agreeing to this, Mary,' he said, showing her his ID. 'We really do appreciate your assistance.'

She ignored the ID and concentrated on his face. 'It all seems very mysterious and – I must confess – rather exciting. When the car turned up at my house I actually felt my heart skip a beat. But you must reassure me about one thing.'

'I'll do my best.'

'By helping you tonight, am I betraying the people I work with?'

'Not at all,' said Charlie, without hesitation. 'Quite the opposite, in fact.' He was about to say more, then checked himself. Mary appraised him with cool, oriental eyes.

'You don't want to tell me very much at all, do you?' she said.

'It's better if I don't.'

'Plausible deniability?'

'Something like that.'

She took a deep breath, then closed the car door quietly behind her. 'All right. If this is as urgent as you say it is, we ought to be getting on with it.'

As the car drove off, Charlie led her back to the trees, where his team was waiting. 'This is Sergeant Johnson. He's covering for Alex until she's back on duty.' As they shook hands, Mary's tiny fingers vanished inside Johnno's enormous fist. Charlie hoped they came out intact. 'And this is Liz Rivers. She's here to ... help things along.'

To her credit, Mary said nothing as she shook hands with Liz. But her eyes took in the black holdall, the tight black trousers and the loose jacket specifically tailored to conceal a shoulder holster. Charlie had considered telling her that Liz worked for MI6, but Liz wouldn't thank him and Mary ... well, if she hadn't guessed something of the sort she was dumber than she looked. And Charlie thought Mary Chen was anything but dumb.

'Did you think about what I said on the phone?' said Charlie, once they'd been introduced.

'How to explain you away, you mean?' said Mary. 'Yes. The story is you've come down from the Aberdeen office, but your plane got in late. You're flying out again in the morning so this is your only chance to see our London operation.'

'So who are we exactly, ma'am?' said Johnno. 'If you don't mind my asking.'

Mary considered the muscles bulging through Johnno's casual jacket and chinos. With the ghost of a smile, she said, 'You're interior designers.'

The front desk was manned by a grizzled security guard. When they came through the revolving doors he was sat with his chin on his hands staring at a portable DVD player. As soon as he saw Mary Chen breezing across the lobby, he stood, the DVD player vanished and his chin aimed itself towards the ceiling.

'Miss Chen,' he said, when they reached the desk. 'Didn't expect to see you back here tonight.' He peered over her shoulder. 'Brought some friends with you?'

'These are some of our colleagues from Scotland,' she replied. She sounded curt. Charlie wondered if this was the voice she used when she told people their services were no longer required. 'They're here to make sure the new extension planned for

Aberdeen conforms to our corporate style. As you can imagine, none of us really wants to be here at one o'clock in the morning, so we'll just do our business as quickly as we can.'

Charlie and the others signed in using a trio of false names provided by Liz Rivers. The security guard studied the opposite wall. When he handed over the visitors' passes his hand was trembling; when they finally left the reception desk, he breathed an audible sigh of relief.

'Is he discreet?' Liz whispered to Mary, as they waited for the lift. 'He seemed a bit edgy.'

'I make Bill nervous,' Mary answered. 'He's got six months to go before he starts drawing a rather generous pension and I'm the one who'll be conducting his exit interview. Trust me – rocking the boat is not on his list of things to do before he retires.'

The lift chimed softly and they all got in. The lift began its ascent to the fifth floor.

'Will there be anyone else around?' asked Charlie.

'Not likely,' said Mary. 'We usually reserve all-nighters for when there's a big tender going through. There may be a few keen ones brown-nosing on the third floor, but

271

they won't disturb you. How long do you need to do ... whatever it is you're going to do?'

'Not long,' said Liz.

The lift doors opened, admitting them into a short, dimly-lit corridor with a T-junction at both ends. Mary led them past a wall of photographs showing Lochavon triumphs from around the world: overground pipe-lines carrying oil through Siberian perma-frost and the Saharan oven; something that looked like a gigantic brewery but was actually a biochemical leaching plant built to extract gold from a Venezuelan mine; tiny electronic widgets that probably did some-thing unfathomable deep underground.

'This looks wacky,' said Johnno, peering at a concept sketch of an unmanned boring vehicle. 'I guess you guys'll do anything to squeeze a buck out of the planet.'

Mary gave him a tolerant smile. 'Whether you like it or not,' she said, 'the planet's resources will be exploited. Lochavon Industries just tries to make it as efficient a process as possible.'

'Won't last forever,' said Johnno, whom Charlie thought made an unlikely environ-mentalist. He wondered if he was due a lecture on the BMW's petrol efficiency...

'Nothing does. Now, if you'd like to follow me – the meeting suite is just down the hall here.'

The Chequer Room was one of three meeting rooms radiating off a central circular lobby. The others were called Stripe and Circle. Curious names. If they were descriptive of the decor, Charlie wondered if they shouldn't *really* hire some interior designers.

The lobby was capped by a glass roof. The moon cast faint shadows across thick carpet and cream leather couches. When Mary flicked on the lights, the shadows disappeared.

'You want I should come in with you, boss?' said Johnno.

'No,' said Charlie. 'Wait out here with Mary. Like Liz said, this part won't take long.'

'Is that why you brought him?' said Mary. 'To keep an eye on me?'

'Extra security,' said Charlie. 'Just in case.'

Mary looked at the two SODs officers, clearly hoping to see a smile. When neither man obliged, her confident façade cracked a little. 'Then you'd better be quick,' she said, sitting abruptly on a couch.

'Don't worry,' said Charlie. 'We will.'

The Chequer Room was startling. The walls were patterned with alternating black and white squares. The furniture was black lacquer; when Charlie turned the lights on, a thousand white highlights kicked off the big meeting table, the glossy bar in the corner, the shelves with their payload of awards and models.

'Jesus Christ,' said Liz. 'It looks like somebody waved the fucking chequered flag.'

'Maybe they like their meetings short,' said Charlie. 'Let's face it – more than ten minutes in here you'd be clawing down the walls. Let's get on with it.'

Liz dropped her holdall on the floor, unzipped it, and flipped open an inner pocket. Inside the pocket was a small black box. The box was the size of a mobile phone and featureless but for a small button and a tiny aerial jutting from one corner.

'Slimbox RSD One-Twenty. This little fucker's got a fourteen-metre range,' she said.

'Is that good?'

She ignored him. 'Only drawback is we need retrieval after the op. Can't leave it lying around for the cleaners to find.'

'Is that a problem?'

Liz regarded him with cool grey eyes. 'We

274

don't do problems.'

Holding the bug like a water diviner, she prowled round the room. She examined the bar. On it was a coffee machine that reminded Charlie of some of the architecture he'd seen outside. She ran her index finger along the edge of one of the display shelves. Finally she dropped to her knees and studied the underside of the table.

She was down there a long time. When she reappeared she was still holding the bug. She tested the strength of the tabletop with her free hand, then leaped lightly on top of it. Her flat shoes made neither a sound nor a mark as she stalked its length, studying the expensive light fittings recessed into the ceiling.

She jumped down again, shaking her head.

'No fucking good,' she said, tossing the bug back in the holdall. From five metres away, her aim was millimetre-perfect.

'Why not?'

'Couldn't say. You'd think this was a science, wouldn't you? But it's not. It's a fucking art.'

A little bemused, Charlie watched as she went back to the holdall and started rummaging. The holdall looked full of stuff, none of which he could identify. He half-expected her to pull out a hat stand. On the other hand, she wasn't exactly Mary Poppins.

When Liz stood up again, she was holding a silver ballpoint pen.

'What's that?' said Charlie.

She rolled her eyes. 'What d'you think? It's a fucking bug. Hasn't got the range of the Slimbox. Battery only lasts twelve hours, but that's all we need. The good news is, we don't have to conceal the fucker.'

Was swearing one of the courses they ran at spy school? If so, he'd give her an 'A' for effort and a 'C' for creative use of vocabulary.

On the bar, beside the designer coffee machine, was a stack of headed notepaper and a white desk tidy. The tidy was full of pens. Liz made a space and stuffed her pen in with the rest.

'Now you see it,' she said. 'Now you don't. What we call "hiding in plain sight".'

'You said it hasn't got the range,' said Charlie. 'Will it pick everything up from over there?'

'Range is nine metres. This room's seven point five on the diagonal. It'll hear. Christ, this fucker's so sensitive it'll pick up the rattle of your bollocks when you put your hands in your pockets.'

'Do you speak from experience?'

'You'd be surprised what I've experienced.'

She fixed Charlie with such a look he decided he'd rather not know any more. He was still trying to work out how she knew the dimensions of the room without actually measuring it.

'Are we done?' he said.

'Nearly.' She rotated the pen's pocket-clip a quarter-turn. 'There. Bug's live. Anything you say from now on may be used against you in a court of law.'

'That's my line. What if someone accidentally turns it off?'

Again the withering look. 'There is no off. Fucker's hot 'til it croaks. After that – it's just a pen.'

The last item she took from the holdall was another black box. This one was bigger – more like a TV remote – and boasted a number of knobs and dials. She connected herself to it with a set of earphones. 'All right – say something.'

'Uh ... testing, one, two, three.'

'Very fucking original. Okay, we're on air. Try it not so loud. And preferably less corny.'

'If I said you had a beautiful body would

you hold it against me?'

'Jesus Christ. Let's get the fuck out of here.'

They returned to the lobby, where Johnno had joined Mary on the couch. He appeared to be regaling her about the merits of red lingerie over white.

'I was just telling Mary here how the wife holds these pantyhose parties,' said Johnno. 'She was real interested.'

Mary stood; the tremor in her shoulders told Charlie she was trying not to laugh. But on her brow there was a light sheen of sweat. Like Liz, she wanted to be gone.

'Have you finished doing ... your thing?' she said.

Charlie put his arm round her and took her aside. 'I think you probably know what our "thing" is,' he said, 'and I want you to know it's okay, really.'

'Is it? It's just that ... oh, I'm used to confidentiality and everything. Part of my job. I don't mind telling you this is taking me a little way out of my comfort zone.' Her eyes studied him. 'Would Alex be telling me the same as you, if she were here?'

'If Alex were here, she'd tell you to do as you're told and not be such a wuss.'

'That sounds like Alex. I do believe I

278

believe you, Chief Inspector Paddon.'

'Charlie. Call me Charlie.' He hesitated. He was thinking about the way Jackie's BA uniform clung to her behind. Then he thought about how Mary Chen's warm laugh melted right through her cool, pro-fessional exterior. 'When all this is cleared up, do you want to meet up for a coffee?'

'So you can tell me what really went on here tonight?'

'I was thinking just coffee.'

'If I say "yes" am I free to go?'

'Uh, not quite. Mary – there's one more thing I need you to do.'

22

June 28th

08:53

Lochavon Industries, Canary Wharf

Charlie stood on the half-mezzanine, leaning on the steel balustrade, overlooking the main lobby. Office workers were pouring in, morning shadows stretched ahead of them like compass pointers. As he scanned the crowed, looking for Malamba, he saw a face he recognised. It wasn't a face he'd expected to see.

Lawrie Chappell had arrived for work.

Charlie watched Lawrie stride across the expensive granite floor. Given that he'd made a special trip from Aberdeen, Charlie realised it was no surprise he'd decided to pay his London colleagues a visit. And with Dubai on the cards, maybe say a few goodbyes.

As Lawrie signed in, Charlie wondered

what Alex – or Danni for that matter – had said to him before he left the house. They both felt he should spend more time with Fraser. He imagined fireworks over the breakfast table.

Lawrie left the desk and went to the lift. Charlie melted to the back of the overhanging floor. It was unlikely he'd be seen, but he couldn't be too careful. As soon as the lift had taken Lawrie away, he was back at the balustrade, watching.

On the wall above the reception desk, a row of five digital clocks displayed the time in different zones around the world. Charlie was only interested in the one in the middle: GMT. That one said it was seven minutes to nine. Any moment now, the revolving door would spin a tall, well-dressed citizen of the Republic of Limpopo into the lobby.

Everything was in place. All he could do was wait.

Mary had found them a small room on the second floor to use as their base.

'Nobody will disturb you in here,' she'd said. 'This whole section's due for a refit so everything's been cleared out. The lights are out but I think the sockets are all live. They're doing major electrical works at the moment – can you believe it, in a building that's only six years old?'

The room was not so much cleared out as gutted. The walls were bare and the furniture consisted of two battered swivel chairs and a disassembled desk. And it was dark. Luckily, although the lights weren't working, one whole wall was glass; once the sun was up the room would be flooded with light.

Charlie and Liz had nodded their approval. Johnno just looked round mournfully and said, 'You think you could arrange a percolator?'

Charlie spent most of the early hours familiarising himself with the layout of the building. Mary showed him round. 'I feel like an air hostess,' she said, as she pointed out yet another fire escape. '"In the event of an emergency, please exit in an orderly fashion along the wing of the aircraft."'

'Hopefully nobody's going to have to escape,' said Charlie, looking through a window at the slowly lightening sky. 'That's why we're here.'

After that, her sense of humour waned. When they got back to the second floor, she excused herself. 'I'm feeling a little like a spare part now. Do you need me for anything else?'

'No, thank you. You've been ... fantastic.'

That lifted the corners of her mouth. 'I hope it's worth it.' She yawned. 'Well, tired as I am, it doesn't look like I'll be getting any sleep tonight. Since I'm here, I might as well do something useful. Any objections if I go to my office and move some paper around?'

'None at all. I'll look in on you before we leave.'

'When will that be?'

Charlie considered this. 'It's hard to say. Depends how things turn out.'

'All right. Good luck.'

Just before six, Brian Burfield and Nick Luard turned up. Mary's final bit of skulduggery had been to book them ahead of time as official visitors. Charlie was waiting to greet them at reception. Both were in their civvies and, to his eyes, stuck out like a pair of thumbs that weren't just sore but plastered and splinted to boot. Or maybe he was just feeling edgy.

Bill the security guard handed out the passes Mary had prepared without a word, then clocked himself out, yawning. He'd either stopped being suspicious or was too tired to care. His place at the desk was taken by a fresh-faced youth with the trace of a French accent, who ignored them completely.

Charlie took Brian and Luard upstairs. They found Liz and Johnno playing Chase the Lady with a pack of cards that looked as if it had been to Baghdad and back. Instead of the usual royal suspects, the picture cards featured photos of lap dancers. Liz didn't seem to mind.

'Welcome to the nerve centre,' Charlie said. Ignoring him, Luard did a quick tour of the room. Apparently satisfied, he took Liz into a corner, where they exchanged a few hushed words.

'Pretty basic accommodation,' said Brian. 'Any tea?'

'There's coffee, sir,' said Johnno, brightly. Brian pulled a face.

Luard asked Liz to show them all the radio receiver.

'It receives and records,' she said, flipping the device in her hand. 'And it's scrambled. It might look simple but there's a lot of Koreans lost their eyesight putting this little fu ... this baby together.'

'I guess there's nothing more we can do,' said Charlie. Brian sighed.

Luard showed them a malicious grin. 'And

you thought spying was a glamorous affair.'

While he waited for Malamba to come through the revolving door, Charlie took one last look around the lobby. The later it got, the more concerned he became. He just hadn't expected it to be so busy.

Lochavon Industries was a big player; naturally that meant a big payroll. What made it worse was that the main parent company rented office space to a number of its subsidiaries. As a result, the lobby at opening time resembled Waterloo Station in rush hour. There were people everywhere: office staff arriving for work, clients and suppliers meeting their early appointments, couriers delivering packages to be signed for, collecting others for delivery. Some of the couriers, Charlie noticed, were directed through a door near the elevators. This door – as he'd discovered during his recce – led not only to the mailroom but to a stairwell running the full height of the building. Using these stairs, you could get all the way from the roof to the basement car park without anybody seeing you. All in all, it was a security nightmare.

Was that the only reason he was feeling uneasy? He couldn't be sure. Alex said only half his hunches were right, but Charlie reckoned that was a pretty good average. He wished Alex were here now. If only he could bounce his thoughts off her, between them they might get to the bottom of this.

Because, despite every theory Henry and Luard had come up with, this whole affair still wasn't adding up. Why did he find it so hard to believe that Malamba was the villain in all this?

Alex's words came back to him: *You like the guy.*

It was true, he supposed. Malamba was quiet and assured – maybe a bit stand-offish. A hard man to get to know. For some reason Charlie felt getting to know him would be worthwhile.

But was he a murderer?

Downstairs, a woman had dropped her briefcase in the revolving door. As she stumbled into the lobby, the door continued to turn, sweeping her case back outside. She threw up her hands in frustration; seconds later, a black man in a slick grey suit emerged from the door with the briefcase in his hand. He dipped his head and presented it to the woman. She had to be at least fifty, but Charlie fancied he could hear her girlish giggle all the way across the lobby.

But the man wasn't Malamba.

Charlie's fingers were gripping the hand-rail so tight his knuckles had turned white. Was it going to be a no-show? Had Malamba somehow got wind of their operation? If so, where would he go? Should they alert the airports?

On the other side of the lobby, a pair of lift doors peeled apart. Paul Malamba emerged. He must have come straight up from the car park. Charlie wondered who he'd got to drive him. They'd put a watch on all the official embassy vehicles.

Malamba crossed the floor to the reception desk. As he lifted the pen to sign his name in the visitor's book, the clock on the wall showing GMT clicked over to 09:00.

Game time.

23

June 28th

09:06

Lochavon Industries, Canary Wharf

A pretty PA took Paul Malamba up to the fifth floor and left him in a slick circular lobby with the promise that Bob Pettifer would meet him shortly. When she had gone, Malamba turned his face up to the glass roof. The sky was pure cobalt, cut through with contrails from a pair of jets soaring high above the world.

He was not alone for long. A door burst open and there was Pettifer, grinning broadly beneath his unmissable hair.

'Paul!' he exclaimed. 'So good to see you again. And on the old home turf too. Well, *my* home at least. I hope you'll treat it like your own.'

'Thank you for agreeing to meet me at such short notice,' said Malamba. Tall as he was, he felt small next to Pettifer. It was not the man but the personality he found over-powering, especially first thing in the morning. 'Shall we proceed?'

'Love to, old man. We're in the Chequer Room. I heard you like chess – thought it might tickle you.'

Malamba followed him into the room, where he was anything but tickled. The decor was hideous, like something out of a night club. He half-expected one of the side doors to admit a bevy of lap dancers. Knowing Pettifer, it was not beyond the realms of possibility.

And yet it *was* like being inside a chess-board. Like being folded up inside a game.

The thought made him shiver.

'Cold?' boomed Pettifer. He fiddled with a control box on the wall. 'I can crank up the heating, even the humidity if you want. Mind you, it's a dry heat down in your neck of the woods. I'll bet you're missing the old African savannah, aren't you?'

'We have little savannah in the Republic,' said Malamba, placing his attaché case on the shiny black table. 'Ours is a country of river and plateau.'

'Righto. Whatever you say. Nice briefcase, by the way. What is it – crocodile? What're you drinking? There's the usual, unless you'd like something stiffer?'

'Nothing, thank you. Can we begin, please?'

'Whatever you say. You're the boss.'

Am I? wondered Malamba. All the way here he had suffered from an increasing sense of foreboding. And now he had arrived ... there was a wildness in Pettifer's eyes that he did not like.

They sat on opposite sides of the table. Paul clicked the locks on his case. Opening it, he withdrew half a dozen folders. Each held a draft agreement for Lochavon Industries to develop various high technology solutions for the Republic of Limpopo's new nationalised mining operation. He placed the folders one on top of the other. Pettifer regarded them greedily.

He pushed the folders to one side.

'Before we discuss these,' he said. 'I wish to talk about something else.'

'Anything you like, Paul. Just as I said: you're...'

'The boss. Yes.'

'So – how d'you want to kick things off?' Pettifer sprawled back in his chair, legs spread, hands clasped behind his head.

Malamba sat very still. 'I wish to begin

with Piet Bakker.'

In the gutted office on the second floor, Charlie leaned closer to the radio receiver.

'They've hardly had time to warm up,' he said, 'and already it's getting interesting.'

'You want I should go up there?' said Johnno. 'I can be outside the door, in case they get frisky.'

'Not yet,' said Brian. 'We'll know when we need to step in.'

A crackle of static burst from the external speaker. Liz – who was monitoring reception via a set of headphones plugged into the back of the receiver – cursed and tweaked one of the knobs.

'I thought these were the latest thing,' said Charlie.

'They are,' she snapped. 'Fucking Koreans.'

'Calmness is your mantra, Rivers,' murmured Nick Luard. As always, he'd seated himself a little apart from the rest, on one of the battered chairs they'd requisitioned from the room next door.

'Yes, sir.' She made another adjustment and the static cleared. 'There – that's got it.'

'Now everybody be quiet, please,' Luard went on. 'As Chief Inspector Paddon has so astutely remarked, this is getting interest-ing.'

Bob Pettifer was speaking again. His voice was loud even through the speaker. Charlie wondered what it sounded like in the meeting room.

'Piet Bakker,' echoed Pettifer. 'Well, what's to say, other than that the old gangster's out of the way for good? And as far as you're concerned, that *is* good, right?'

'His death has removed certain ... obstacles,' said Malamba, slowly.

'Exactly right,' said Pettifer, 'Look, you and I haven't known each other very long, but we've already got, well, an *understanding*. Now we've spent some time together, I'm more than confident we're on the same wavelength. Aren't you?'

'Go on.'

Pettifer tipped his chair back and filled a paper cup from the water cooler behind him. He drained the cup, scrunched and tossed it in the waste bin.

'I daresay you know all about what Bakker and Kissonga used to get up to behind the scenes.' He winked. 'Bet you had a finger in the pie yourself, eh? Well, now it's just the two of us, I don't mind putting my cards on the table, not now we're going to be doing business together. It's like this: over the years, Bakker shifted a lot of capital around, most of it through the UK. Through Scotland, if you want to be more exact. If you want to be even more exact – through Lochavon Industries, or one of its many subsidiaries. Am I telling you anything you hadn't already guessed?'

'Please, do continue,' said Malamba. He was having to keep his hands flat on the table to stop them shaking, because the fact was, up until this moment, he had had no idea Pettifer had been Bakker's British contact. None whatsoever. He had chosen to work with Lochavon Industries purely on the strength of their reputation. The name Lochavon Industries had not come up once in over thirty years of trade between the Republic of Limpopo and the rest of the world. Kissonga and Bakker had covered their tracks like professionals. Which was exactly what they were.

Professional thieves.

How can I have been so naive?

'So, when your department contacted me wanting to set up meetings, I obliged. Only natural you should want to ... well, shall we say, "follow in the footsteps of your predecessors"? It's a clever cover you've come up with, I have to say – all this technological research malarkey. I've got to say, it's genius. It'll give the whole thing a credibility it never had before. Save some fancy footwork – and I've had to do plenty of that in my time, believe me!'

'I believe you,' murmured Malamba.

Pettifer was warming to his subject now. He stood, cracked his knuckles and started pacing up and down. His reflection moved with him, cold and clean in the polished surface of the table.

'Once we've got the tech agreements in place, we'll arrange a few more of these tête-à-têtes, just the two of us. Work out the best way to move everything else forward. I personally favour off-shore investments, but I daresay you've got your own favourites. You'll have to invite me to the Republic of Limpopo – I fancy shooting a few water buffalo or whatever it is you have down there. Get myself one of those fancy brief-cases.'

'The way I see it, now we've cancelled Bakker's account, we're free to write our own cheques.'

Malamba was mesmerised by the sight of Pettifer stalking back and forth in front of the black and white tiles on the wall. It really was like a chessboard, he decided. What did that make Pettifer? Not a knight, certainly – there was nothing noble about this man. Nor a rook.

A bishop. He comes at you on the diagonal, like the blade of a knife slicing where you least expect it.

'You use the word "we" a great deal,' he said. 'This is, perhaps, the time to point out that no contract has yet been signed. This is still a negotiation.'

'Of course. But we're men of the world – you know as well as I do you don't need paper to make a contract. All you need is two people in agreement, over drinks say. Just a handshake, old man, that's all it takes.'

'Well, yes, but the papers I have prepared...'

'Are a formality. The hard work's already been done.'

'Forgive me.' Malamba felt the conversation slipping from him. At the same time, his sense of dread was increasing. 'When you say "hard work"...'

'Getting rid of Bakker. Bit of a SNAFU first time round, of course. If he hadn't tripped on the steps like that we'd have nailed him with the first shot. Shame that little WPC caught the bullet. Still, there's more than one way to skin a cat. We cracked it in the end. Anyway, with Bakker out of the way, it'll be the easiest thing in the world to shunt all the arrangements I had with him over to you. Paul – you'll soon be the richest man in the Republic of Limpopo. And if your projections about the cobalt reserves are on the ball, before very much longer you'll be the richest man in Africa!'

'You killed Bakker,' said Malamba, very quietly.

Pettifer tipped him a salute. 'Just following orders.'

'*Orders?*'

'I like your style, Paul. Can't be too careful, even here, let alone in a public place like Ye Grapes. Never know who might be watching.'

Malamba could feel the blood draining from his head. Any minute now he was going to faint. He wanted to throw himself back from the table, vomit on the carpet, scream at this wild-eyed murderer that he had got it all wrong – everything from who Paul Malamba was to what drove him on.

'You thought I...' he began, but then his mouth dried up and he could say no more.

Somehow he brought himself under control. He stared past Pettifer at the squares on the wall. He imagined chess pieces sliding from one square to the next, forming ranks, advancing.

Pettifer filled two more cups with water. Holding one, he pushed the other across the table to Malamba. 'Relax,' he said. 'The job's done. Time to move on. Let's drink a toast. To Africa!'

Gradually Malamba's heartbeat slowed; the feeling of dizziness subsided.

'Bring me a pen,' he said, ignoring the offered drink. 'And I will show you exactly what Africa means to me.'

Liz pulled the headphones off.

'What the fuck was that?' she yelled.

'Keep calm,' said Luard.

'Fuck calm. Someone just put a pickaxe through my fucking ear!'

They listened to the grinding noise coming through the speaker. It sounded like a never-ending car crash.

'Something wrong with your equipment, Nick?' said Brian.

'Nothing's wrong,' said Luard. 'But it would appear that one of the surveillance subjects has just picked up our pen.'

Fighting to keep his hand steady, Malamba sketched a rough map of Africa. Pettifer watched with his arms folded and a half-smile on his face.

Malamba partitioned off the bottom of the map with a straggly line. 'South Africa,' he said. Inside this partition he drew a tiny circle. 'Lesotho.' He continued north, out-lining Namibia, Zambia, Zimbabwe ... until finally, wedged between the borders of South Africa and Botswana, he drew an inverted triangle. Finally he inked in the triangle so that it stood out solid black against his pale sketch of the rest of the African continent.

He put down the pen and held up the paper.

'What do you see?'

'The Republic of Limpopo, of course. I do know my geography.'

'Exactly. Then you see what I see. When-ever I look at Africa, I see the Republic. When I wake, I see it. All I do, Mr Pettifer, I do for my family and my country. It is all I have ever done, and will ever do. If I have led you to believe otherwise, then I am surely damned, because that has led to the death of a man who, for all his crimes, did not deserve to be murdered. Nevertheless, my intentions remain as they always have: to serve my country. Whatever "special arrangements" you once made with Piet Bakker are none of my concern. In fact, I now doubt whether Lochavon Industries can deliver on the promises it has made to make the Republic of Limpopo's mines profitable *for its people.*' He stood from the table. 'This meeting is at an end.'

Pettifer stood immobile, arms folded. Red blotches were rising in his cheeks. 'I don't open my doors to just anyone, you know,' he said. 'Don't forget you're a visitor in my company. Hell, you're a visitor in my whole fucking *country!*'

'Which means,' said Malamba, 'that I can do what any other visitor can do: walk away.' He started dropping the folders back into his case.

'You don't want to do that. When I shut doors they stay shut.'

'It seems to me you have a great deal more to lose here than I do, Mr Pettifer. Lochavon Industries is just one of many on my list of possible partners. Or should I say, "was"?' He clicked the case shut, fumbling as his fingers trembled on the clasps.

'After all I've done for you people...'

'I believe that everything you do, you do

for yourself.'

'You go now, you'll regret it.'

'I will find my own way out. Good day, Mr Pettifer.'

He turned and made for the door.

Even Nick Luard had crowded in on the receiver. There had been a frantic few seconds as Liz had adjusted the gain to compensate for the fumbling of Malamba's fingers on the microphone. Then the signal cleared anyway, and they all agreed he'd put the pen down again. With the bug less than a metre away from his face, Malamba's voice came through as though they were all in the same room.

Charlie watched Luard's expression grow more and more thunderous as it became clear he'd been wrong all along. Seeing the head of MI6 drop the ball definitely qualified as a guilty pleasure. Just as satisfying was the knowledge that his own hunch had been proved right. Unfortunately, both were overshadowed by his growing concern for Paul Malamba's safety. Given that Pettifer had just confessed to murdering Piet Bakker on the strength of a misinterpreted conversation in a Mayfair pub, Charlie wondered what he'd be capable of when his blood was up.

The conversation in the Chequer Room had ended. He held his breath, listening with the others. Liz turned up the gain but they heard nothing. Had Malamba left the room or not? What was going on in there?

The seconds ticked by, too many of them.

'We've got to get Malamba out of there,' said Charlie. He leaped to his feet, shoving his chair backwards across the room. 'Right now.'

24

June 28th

09:34

Lochavon Industries, Canary Wharf

Charlie was halfway to the door when Johnno said, 'Hold up!'

Johnno might not have been Alex, but he was the next best thing.

'Make it quick, Johnno,' he said.

'Listen.'

More sounds were coming from the receiver: footsteps, fast and quiet; a phone being lifted from its cradle; a muffled voice.

'What's he saying?' said Brian.

'Shh,' said Liz. She clamped the headphones tight, straining to hear. 'It's Pettifer. I think he's using the phone on the bar. I can't make out what he's saying ... wait a second ... something "park"?'

She raised her eyebrows and looked – not at Luard, as Charlie would have expected –

but straight at Charlie. Suddenly he knew what she was thinking.

'Johnno!' he snapped. 'Get up to the fifth floor. Try and intercept Pettifer before he leaves the meeting room.'

They reached the door at the same time. For all his bulk, Johnno moved like a cat. 'You'll be where, boss?'

'Basement. Keeping talking to me.'

'You got it.'

While Johnno headed up the stairs, Charlie raced down the corridor. He ran straight past the lifts. Lifts had a mind of their own: however hard you pushed the buttons, they always went the wrong way – and took their own sweet time about it. Rounding the corner at the end, he crashed through an anonymous-looking door and on to the service staircase. These were the stairs he'd observed from the elevated floor overlooking the lobby. The stairs that led straight down to the basement car park.

He took them two at a time, cursing all the way. Why hadn't they made camp in one of the adjacent rooms? At the time, the risk of discovery had seemed too great. Now, with Paul Malamba's life in the hands of a man who thought nothing of shooting police officers or cutting throats in the middle of

London, he wished they'd taken the chance.

Johnno will nab Pettifer, he told himself. *All I need to do is reach Malamba first.*

He'd already passed a stainless steel number '1' on the stairwell wall; now he skidded past a large letter 'G'. One more flight to go.

The lights were out on the final stretch. The bloody electrical refit. Charlie grabbed the handrail, whipped round the last dog-leg and stopped just short of the door to the car park. His Glock 17 handgun was in its holster at his waist. He drew it.

Some officers, he knew, said a prayer whenever they 'went live'. Charlie always tried to keep emotions and firearms on separate channels. The gun was just a tool – it would do only what he told it. The best advice he'd had on the subject had come from Brian Burfield: 'Clear head beats hot head, every time.'

With both hands on the grip and the barrel pointing at the ceiling, Charlie gently shouldered the door open.

The light wasn't much better here in the car park. Emergency sodiums flashed fitful yellow shadows from one concrete pillar to the next. The ceiling coffers pressed low; Charlie could feel the weight of the whole building above his head. It stank of exhaust fumes.

Actually it was just this end of the basement in darkness. Further away, beyond the wasp-striped edge of an emergency shutter, the rest of the car park was flooded with light. A Land Rover Discovery was moving slowly through the glare, its driver clearly seeking a parking space. All the bays in the lit area were taken. Here in the Twilight Zone, several were empty.

Find a space fast. Charlie tried to project his thoughts out to the Discovery's driver. *Just don't come down here.*

He thumbed the call button on his radio. 'Johnno,' he whispered. 'Where are you?' There was no reply. 'Johnno? Report.'

Still no reply. *Shit.*

Sudden movement caught his eye. He turned, snapped out his arms. The Glock pointed into the shadows behind a black Lexus. The yellow lamp behind the car sputtered and the darkness moved. His finger tensed on the trigger. But there was nothing there. Like Charlie, the shadows were twitchy.

He lifted the barrel again, huddled back into the darkness by the stairwell door, made himself invisible. Scanned the rows of parked vehicles. Most were big saloons or four-by-fours. Executive rides. For all the problems with the electrics, this was the bigwigs' parking area. Sure enough, on the wall behind the parked cars was a series of nameplates: *CEO, Finance Director, HR Director...* The Lexus was in the CEO's space. Pettifer's car. Beside it was a set of lift doors marked 'Private'.

Further along, near a set of fire shutters, the cars got scruffier. One in particular caught his eye: a white Peugeot with a dented front wing. There was a man behind the wheel, apparently asleep. Beside it was an empty space.

The Discovery slipped under the fire shutter and reversed into the space. Something about it looked familiar.

A shape rose from behind one of the concrete pillars halfway along the row of cars: Paul Malamba, the Republic of Limpopo Minister for Minerals. He set off towards the Peugeot. So that was how he'd got here. Charlie wondered who the driver was. He also began to wonder if he really was asleep. His head was tipped back at a rather alarming angle.

Malamba waited while the driver of the Discovery got out. It was a small blonde woman. Danni the nanny. She smiled at

Malamba and he smiled back. Charlie watched in disbelief as she opened the passenger door and unbuckled Fraser from his booster seat. What the hell were they doing here?

Then he remembered Danni telling him how keen Alex was that Lawrie should make the most of his visit to London – see as much of Fraser as he could. When Lawrie had come to the office this morning, Alex must have told Danni to follow him and pay a surprise visit. After all, what little boy wouldn't want to sit in his daddy's big leather chair and play with the phones?

His eyes strayed back to the Peugeot. Suddenly he realised what it was about the car that made him uneasy. It wasn't the battered wing. It wasn't even the way the driver was slumped in a way no sleeping man would sit.

It was the small black box half-hidden under the wheel arch.

Charlie shoved himself away from the wall. He tried to sprint, but his body was moving as if through treacle. In contrast, his thoughts were racing. He was imagining his second visit to Alex's sick bed. The visit where he told her that, because he'd screwed up again, her son and his nanny had ended up smeared across the ceiling of an underground car park at Canary Wharf.

Malamba and Danni had swapped places. While Danni hoisted Fraser on to her hip and fussed with her bag, Malamba started tugging at the Peugeot's passenger door. But it wouldn't open. He bent to peer in through the window. 'Toby!' he shouted. 'Toby!' He banged on the window. Danni stared past him at the driver, open-mouthed.

'Get back!' bellowed Charlie, as he ran towards them. 'Paul! Danni! There's a bomb under the car – get back now!'

Malamba took a clumsy step backwards. He was looking wildly round. When he spotted Charlie, he bolted for an emergency exit on the other side of the shutters. Charlie imagined briefly what Malamba must have seen: a burly man in a bullet-proof vest bearing down on him with weapon drawn and a crazed look on his face. No wonder he ran.

Danni, however, had frozen. Charlie wondered if she'd even recognised him. Rounding the nose of the Discovery, he holstered his gun and threw his arm around her. She was shaking. In her arms, Fraser looked remarkably calm. Charlie threw a quick glance in Malamba's direction – was the doorway beyond the bomb's blast radius? He thought so. Danni and Fraser, however, were most definitely not.

Nor was the Peugeot's driver. Charlie spared a second to look inside. It was Toby, the fat doorman from the embassy. As he'd suspected, Toby wasn't asleep. The reason his head was tilted at that awkward angle was because his throat had been cut. Just like Bakker's.

'Ch-Charlie?' said Danni. 'What's going on?'

'No time. This way.'

'But I haven't locked the...'

'Move it!'

He holstered his gun and hustled her back to the stairwell, heaved the door open and shoved her through.

'Whatever you do,' he said, 'don't come out!' She looked ready to cry. Fraser, incredibly, was giggling. In his left hand he held one of the Matchbox cars he'd been playing with in Alex's hall.

Charlie let the door swing shut. Out in the car park, Malamba had reached the fire-exit and sank to the ground in the doorway and hugged his knees, looking terrified.

'Get out!' Charlie shouted. Malamba didn't respond.

Charlie's veins were fizzing with adrenalin. The guy was too scared to move. He had to get to Malamba, make him safe. But this was no time for haste. Whoever had killed Toby and planted the bomb might still be around.

He held himself still, took a deep breath, gave his heart a direct order to slow down. Without waiting for it to obey, he drew his gun again and started creeping along the row of cars towards Malamba.

He'd covered less than ten metres when a woman's voice shouted, 'Paddon! Three o'clock!'

The voice was followed instantly by a colossal bang. *Bomb!* he thought. He tucked and rolled, all the time expecting to be showered with chunks of Peugeot. But the Peugeot didn't budge. At which point, Charlie realised what it was he'd heard: *gunshot!*

Coming out of the roll, he whipped the Glock to his right. There was another explosion. Concrete dust sprayed from the doorway where Malamba was huddled. Behind the Lexus, one of the shadows moved, resolved itself into the shape of a man. The shadow was misshapen, elongated – the man was carrying a rifle.

Another explosion, and a star-flash of light

from the rifle's muzzle. Malamba rolled over, flat on the ground. Was he hit?

Charlie opened fire. He let the Glock kick, each time bringing its muzzle down before loosing the next round. He pumped three bullets into the darkness. The man with the rifle stumbled, fell back against the wall, rebounded without a sound. The rifle clattered to the floor. The shooter took two faltering steps forward into a pool of sickly yellow light, revealing his face in profile – sharp nose, weak chin. Not a face Charlie knew. Then, from somewhere behind Charlie, came two more gunshots. The man's head snapped back and he sprawled across the boot of the Lexus.

Charlie held his breath, flicked his gaze from fallen rifleman to empty doorway and back again. He had no clue where the second volley of shots had been fired from. The basement echoes had both amplified and dispersed the sound. Who else was shooting down here?

Something touched his shoulder.

He whipped round, jammed the Glock's barrel into the ribs of the person who'd crept up on him without making a sound. He'd drawn the trigger halfway back before recognition came.

'Liz!' he breathed. 'What the hell are you doing?'

'Sorry, pal. Elementary mistake. Don't sneak up on the good guys. Looks like I need another fucking term at spy school.'

'Where did you come from?'

'Stairs. Don't worry. Girl and the kid are okay.'

She'd taken off her jacket, revealing a black sweater as tight as her trousers. Her shoulder holster gripped her torso. Her expression was a startling mix of grimness and vivacity.

'You fired those shots?' said Charlie.

'Who else?'

'Malamba!'

'He's okay – look.'

Malamba had lifted his head from the ground and was looking cautiously around. He gave Charlie a faltering thumbs up.

'We've got to get him clear,' said Charlie.

'He's safe for now – let's check our sharpshooter's out of commission first.'

The rifleman was dead. It looked like Charlie's shots had smashed most of his ribs. Liz's had removed most of his face.

'Recognise him?' she said, delving into his jacket.

Charlie shook his head. 'Even his mother

wouldn't know him now.'

'Abel Horwitz,' said Liz, flipping open a wallet. 'Full-time finance director and part-time assassin.' She delved again and came up with a small black box that could have come out of her holdall. 'Remote detonator. Reckon Horwitz took out the driver, then rigged the car so he could blow it as soon as Malamba got near. Only the woman turned up with the kid and put him off. Lucky for us the fucker had a conscience.'

Poor Toby, thought Charlie sadly. Malamba had done the big doorman a favour by playing courier between him and his brother. What loyal employee wouldn't repay the compliment by doing a little unofficial chauffeuring when the need arose? Except his loyalty had got him killed.

'Let's get Malamba the hell out of here,' he said.

'Roger that,' said Liz. 'But nice and fucking easy. I don't like surprises.'

As they circled the Lexus, Charlie's radio crackled into life.

'Charlie?' came a voice. It was Johnno. 'You there, buddy?'

'I'm here. Where are you?'

'Second floor. Bastard cold-conked me.'

Charlie glanced at Liz. They were inching

313

forward, their movements matched step for step.

'Where is he now?' he said into the radio.

'Dunno,' said Johnno.

'Call Brian and security,' said Charlie. 'Seal access to the car park, evacuate the building.'

'Roger than,' said Johnno.

At that moment, the private lift doors slid open, revealing a bright interior. A figure emerged and ran, crouched low, between the line of parked cars and the concrete wall. For a second he looked in their direction. Charlie saw two things that made his heart step up a gear: the pistol in the man's hand and the look of animal fury on his face.

'Pettifer!' said Liz.

Both Charlie and Liz aimed their hand-guns, but Pettifer was already out of sight.

They froze, waiting, gun barrels tracking the gloom. Above their heads, a ventilation fan coughed into life. Cool air wafted over them. The draught plucked a Mars bar wrapper from under the Lexus's front tyre and sent it skipping away down the length of the car park.

Silently, Charlie waved his hand towards the lift. Liz nodded. She left his side and crept round the Lexus. The lift doors hissed shut, erasing the light and wrapping her in darkness.

Alone now, Charlie inched towards Malamba, all the time keeping his eyes on the dark tract behind the vehicles, waiting for Pettifer to make his move.

At the other end of the car park, a car engine roared into life. Seconds later, a white BMW eased out of its parking space and disappeared up the exit ramp, its driver oblivious to the drama unfolding in the distant shadows. The overhead fan whined to a halt. Silence once more.

'Pettifer!' shouted Charlie. 'Armed police! We have you surrounded. Put down your weapon and come out with your hands up.'

Still Pettifer didn't show himself. Bent double, Charlie continued to move towards Malamba. Just ten metres to go, then they'd be out of the fire exit and in the clear. He deliberately scuffed his boots on the ground, keeping out of sight but making enough noise to let Pettifer know where he was. Giving Liz a chance to creep up on him from behind. They needed back-up – they were woefully short of bodies.

'There's nowhere to go, Pettifer. Put the gun down and come out where we can see you!'

He covered another five metres. Where the hell was Pettifer?

Malamba was edging away from the doorway, coming to meet him. *Shit, no!* Charlie motioned at him to get back.

Pettifer stepped out from behind the Discovery.

A lithe black figure – Liz – raced towards him in total silence.

'Freeze!'

But Pettifer was faster than a grey-haired CEO had any right to be. He spun on his heel and fired. The MI6 agent pulled her trigger, too. Liz grunted and fell backwards, crashing against the wall and dropping into the darkness. Pettifer swivelled around. Charlie thought it was the recoil from the shot, but then he saw that he was clutching his shoulder.

'Fucking bitch!' said Pettifer, through his teeth. He steadied himself and walked calmly round the Discovery to where Malamba had just planted himself square in his sights.

Charlie already had the Glock levelled at Pettifer. He squeezed the trigger.

There was nothing but a dry click. *No!* He squeezed once more. Another click. He dropped the gun and dashed towards Malamba, pushing him towards a fire door.

He slammed into the metal bar. It didn't budge.

'Oh dear,' said Pettifer, staggering forwards, blood seeping between his fingers from the injured shoulder. 'I must get the service team to look at that.'

Charlie scrambled in front of Malamba, using himself as a shield.

'Is this all they teach you people?' said Pettifer. 'Getting in the way?'

He raised his gun. Charlie thought of Alex.

The sound of the gunshot was deafening.

Charlie ducked, but there was no impact. Instead, a cloud of blood exploded from Pettifer's hip. He staggered sideways, his mouth open in shock. A second shot and his hand disintegrated. His pistol flew sideways and skidded across the ground, with the mess that was his fingers. Screaming, he sank to his knees. Blood spurted from his ruined hand. A third shot hit him in the left side of his neck, and he collapsed on to his back. His arm flapped twice on the ground, then was still. The CEO of Lochavon Industries wouldn't be making any more deals.

Charlie heard footsteps. Someone was walking towards him from the brighter end of the car park. He circled to crouch on

317

Malamba's opposite side, shielding him against any further attack.

For a second, the figure was just a silhouette. Then one of the faulty fluorescents finally kicked in and the area was bathed in light, revealing Nick Luard, impeccably dressed and holding a vintage Colt.

'There's no need to look so surprised, Charlie,' Luard said. 'I wasn't always a desk jockey, you know.' He blew away the smoke still trailing from the muzzle of the Colt. 'You should ask for a real gun, by the way – you obviously can't trust those plastic toys of yours in a crisis.'

Charlie was still formulating a response when the stairwell doors burst open and Sergeant Jeff Johnson came staggering out. One side of his face was caked with blood.

'Did I miss the party?' he said. Charlie snapped back to his senses.

'Liz,' said Charlie. 'She's been shot. Johnno, that Peugeot's hot – alert the bomb disposal team. Nick, get Malamba out.'

Nick Luard was already escorting Malamba back to the stairwell. Johnno got on the radio. Charlie ran towards Liz. Expecting the worst, he was pleased to see she was sitting up, her back against the Discovery and her right hand pressed against her left side. Her fingers were crimson with blood.

'Are you okay?' said Charlie, dropping to one knee.

'Course I'm not fucking okay. Fucker shot me.'

'I can see that. Can you move?'

'You fucking help me, I'll fucking move. What about our man?'

'Malamba's safe. Pettifer's down.'

Liz grimaced, her features pale, as he helped her to her feet. 'One up for the boys in blue?'

'I'd love to claim the prize but I have to admit it was your boss who took him out.'

Liz stared at him in astonishment. She seemed lost for words.

Charlie nodded. ''Fraid so.'

'Shit. I'll never hear the last of this. Come on – I've got a burning desire to acquaint myself with a large bandage and an even larger fucking Scotch.'

The others were waiting for them through the doors at the bottom of the stairs.

'Bomb disposal's on its way,' said Johnno. 'Paramedics are coming in the front.' He turned to Liz. 'Think you can make one flight of stairs?'

'Try and fucking stop me.'

Charlie turned to Paul Malamba.

'Sir, I think you should come with me now,' he said. 'There's still an explosive device wired to that car and I'd feel happier if you were somewhere else.'

Malamba stood, brushed himself down and straightened his jacket. He stared with undisguised contempt at Bob Pettifer, who lay on the blood-stained concrete with both eyes wide open.

'Do you know something, Officer Paddon?' he said. 'So would I.'

25

July 1st

12:09

SODs Headquarters, New Scotland Yard

Henry Worthington paused outside the meeting room door. His list of pet hates – if itemised – would probably run to several pages. Being late would be somewhere near the top. The illusion of control, that was the key. Just because he'd decided to walk the short distance to Scotland Yard from Whitehall, and been forced by the ever-expanding sewer repairs to divert round what felt like six city blocks under a sun that was trying to barbecue the back of his neck in air that felt like a sauna ... well, it didn't give him an excuse to look flustered.

He pushed open the door and marched in.

'Bit late, aren't we, Henry?' said Brian Burfield, tapping his cheap watch with something close to a smile. Sitting next to him was a young woman in a yellow blouse; on the opposite of the meeting table were Charlie Paddon and Nick Luard.

'Sincere apologies,' said Henry, draping his jacket on the back of a chair. 'One or two things came up, needed my attention. You know how it is. Can't let the big machine grind to a halt.'

'Hot out there, is it?'

Suddenly conscious of the damp patches under his arms, Henry slipped his jacket back on again. 'Are you providing lunch?' he said. 'I hope you're still using those new caterers. They were certainly a step in the right direction.'

'Sorry to disappoint,' said Burfield. 'Some trouble over seafood. Health and Safety shut them down. Back to pork pies, I'm afraid.'

Henry took out his handkerchief and dabbed his brow. 'What a pity,' he said.

'Don't worry, Henry,' said the woman in the yellow blouse. 'There are cakes too.'

He suddenly recognised Alex Chappell. 'Do forgive me, my dear,' he said. 'I didn't recognise you in your clothes – I mean without your uniform on.' He stopped, started again. 'What I'm trying to say is: it's good to see you up and about.'

'It suits me too, sir,' said Alex. 'There's only so much daytime television a woman can take.'

'I imagine there is. Well...' he clapped his hands together '...I believe this brings us to the first item on the agenda, namely Sergeant Chappell's heroic actions outside the Republic of Limpopo Embassy a few days ago. I had a word with the Home Secretary only yesterday and he confirmed everything. There's still some paperwork to be done but I can tell you now, Alex, that you look likely to receive nothing less than the Queen's Gallantry Medal. On behalf of the department may I be the first to offer you my warmest congratulations.'

Burfield seconded this with a 'hear hear' that was somehow more heartfelt for being grunted under his breath. Nick Luard nodded politely – one professional to another – while Paddon positively beamed.

'Thank you, sir,' said Alex. 'All I did was get shot.'

'Occupational hazard of being partnered with Chief Inspector Paddon here,' said Nick Luard. 'As Agent Rivers will testify.'

To his credit, Charlie kept his cool. 'How's Liz doing, Nick?' he said.

'The bullet chipped a rib,' said Luard, 'but

she's a tough girl. She'll be back on duty next week.'

'Like I said,' said Alex, coolly, 'it's either that or watching cheap chat shows.'

'Well,' said Henry, keen to keep the meeting light and upbeat, 'all's well that ends well. I'm sure we're all looking forward to seeing you receive your well-deserved award, Alex.'

'Thank you, sir,' Alex said.

'At least we won't have to drag you back from the Middle East to receive it. I gather your relocation plans are on permanent hold?'

Alex glanced at Paddon, whose eyebrows had just shot up. It was amusing watching the interchange between them. Clearly she hadn't brought her colleagues up to date.

'For those of us who weren't aware,' Henry elaborated, 'following the deaths of Bob Pettifer and Abel Horwitz, Lochavon Industries is undergoing what one might call a "radical restructuring". Part of the fallout from this is that Alex's husband Lawrie is now no longer in line for transfer to Dubai. Given the shake-up, however, I understand a promotion may be on the cards for him?'

He addressed this last to Alex herself, who was squirming in her chair. Henry supposed she felt like he was washing her laundry in public. But it was worth it to see the flip-book of emotions running across Charlie Paddon's face.

'Can we move on?' said Luard. He was slumped in his chair, uncharacteristically glum.

'Still licking your wounds, Nick?' said Burfield. This was quite an about-turn, Henry thought, with Burfield cracking the jokes (well, as near to jokes as he could get) and Luard glowering in the corner.

'I don't know what you mean,' said Luard.

'I mean Paul Malamba turning out to be the golden boy after all, not the vengeful money-grabber you thought he was. All the time you thought he was feathering his own nest, he was building bridges for his country. Quite the patriot, that chap. I don't know how you got it so wrong. So much for intelligence.'

By the time he'd finished, Burfield was actually smiling. Henry stifled a laugh. Alex raised her hand to her mouth to hide what was surely a grin.

'Although we shouldn't forget,' said Charlie, 'that it was Nick who took out Pettifer just as he was about to put a bullet between Paul Malamba's eyes.'

They all stared at him, unable to believe a SODs officer had leaped to the defence of MI6. Even Luard looked stunned.

'Yes, of course,' said Henry quickly, 'well done, indeed. A very satisfactory outcome to what turned out to be a rather complicated situation.'

There was a knock at the door. Burfield opened it, admitting a chubby constable with a rattling trolley bearing lunch. The sandwiches were already curling at the edges. Balanced on top was a rather tired-looking pork pie.

Henry sighed.

'I thought you might appreciate an update on our Limpopo friends,' he said, as the constable abandoned them to the dubious feast. 'As you know, after concluding their eventful visit to our shores, President Saiki and Paul Malamba flew straight to Washington DC where, I'm sure, our colonial cousins welcomed them with open arms. After Malamba's failure to secure the technology he was chasing in the UK, I suspect he'll be enjoying the hospitality of any number of mining conglomerates keen to sell him the very latest American gadgets. I understand his wife and children will be flying out to join him. They're hoping to spend a few days in Florida before the whole family returns home.'

He paused. It was nearly the school holidays. He wondered what Jack and Mary had planned for the boys. Maybe it was time he took his nephews to Disneyland.

'Speaking of holidays...' He extracted a piece of paper from his folder and slid it across the table to Alex. She skimmed through it, eyes widening. 'What you're reading is an official invitation from President Saiki for you, Alex, and your family to spend a week in the Republic of Limpopo. All expenses paid, of course. In recognition of your gallantry, you are to be guest of honour at the ceremony to open a new cobalt mine near the Mokatse Plateau. I understand they'll be throwing in a safari as well.'

'That's fantastic,' said Alex. Her eyes were shining. 'I mean– it's a great honour.'

'Shame you'll have to pass on the safari,' said Luard. When the others stared at him he elaborated, 'Police officers aren't permitted to accept gifts.'

'Bollocks,' said Burfield, wrestling with the tea urn on the back of the trolley. 'The girl's going and that's that.'

'Looks like you're getting that trip abroad after all,' said Charlie.

'But at least I'll be coming back.'

Brian Burfield filled mugs and handed them round. It wasn't exactly jasmine, but Henry was thirsty enough not to care. Noticing the chip in the rim, he transferred hands and sipped from the other side.

'I think you'll agree it's been a bumpy one,' said Burfield. 'Would have been a lot bumpier if we hadn't had these two on the case. So here's a toast. To Charlie Paddon and Alex Chappell – the best couple of SODs in the business!'

Everyone raised their mugs. Nick Luard even raised a smile. Outside the window, the sun beat down. Henry glanced down his agenda and saw the names of seventeen foreign diplomats due to arrive in the UK over the next fortnight. Summer was well and truly here.

Burfield reached past him and grabbed a handful of cheese and pickle sandwiches. 'Better not hang about, Henry,' he said, 'or it'll all be gone.'

When in Rome, thought Henry.

He helped himself to a pork pie.

Epilogue

August 4th

Mokatse Mine, Republic of Limpopo

Jack McClintock's muse was working overtime. Maybe it was relief that all that Piet Bakker business was over with. Or maybe it was just the beautiful surroundings. He couldn't imagine a more stunning location for a cobalt mine. Or for anything at all, really.

The new mine was located under the sheer east wall of the Mokatse Plateau. The wall rose nearly two thousand feet before levelling abruptly to form a vast elevated plain. A huge waterfall poured from the rich green forest overhanging its edge, raising clouds of spray into the African sunlight.

Square in front of this magical landscape was the Mokatse Mine visitor centre. The bone-shaped building looked like something out of Jurassic Park and was, in Jack's opinion, the master stroke. Within a year this place would have a themed underground tour and a dozen state-of-the-art rides; as well as flooding the world market with affordable cobalt, this former backwater looked set to become the coolest place to visit since Walt Disney decided to move from two dimensions to three.

Historically, wrote Jack, *the Limpopo plateaux have been easy to defend, impossible to attack, and are one of the reasons this tiny nation has maintained its identity during the turbulence of the nineteenth and twentieth centuries. First the Zulus, then the Voortrekkers occupied it. Each time the people of the Limpopo retreated to their castles in the clouds and pulled up the drawbridges.*

Now the plateaux were looking after their people again.

Opinion is divided as to where Sir Arthur Conan Doyle drew his inspiration for The Lost World. Most authorities hold that it was Venezuela, but the great writer is known to have visited the area on at least two occasions and, standing beneath the mighty Mokatse Plateau, one can almost hear the roar of the dinosaurs.

He read it back. A touch of hyperbole? Maybe. But this whole party was over the top. He'd just watched a performance by six hundred tribal dancers dressed in the brightest costumes he'd ever seen. Soon there would be fireworks.

Jack was watching the show from the middle tier of a grandstand erected specifically for just this event. He was surrounded by members of the press from all around the world. Considering this was essentially a local story, there was an incredible amount of international interest. After the drama of Saiki's London visit – and the extraordinary publicity he'd garnered by doing the Time Warp with America's First Lady at a presidential dinner-dance – the Republic of Limpopo was basking in the spotlight.

And loving every minute of it.

The irrepressible Mani Saiki arrived in his newly acquired presidential Rolls Royce and ascended the steps to the stage. He was surrounded by scantily clad girls and greeted by thunderous applause. Jack tried to pick out the security guards and saw just three. It was incredible how relaxed it all was, given that they still had no idea who was behind the assassination attempt at the bridge back in June. Kissonga still had plenty of supporters at large – the bomb could have been planted by any one of them. Perhaps they would never know the answer. One thing was for sure: it wasn't going to spoil the fun.

331

That was one more thing he loved about this country: they embraced their fear rather than hiding behind it.

Saiki's speech was joyous and overblown, much like the man delivering it. The crowd lapped it up. Once he'd finished, Saiki announced that it was time for the official opening and introduced his guest of honour: Alex Chappell, the SODs sergeant who'd taken a bullet for him outside the embassy in London back in June. Well, actually the bullet had been aimed at Piet Bakker, but who was quibbling?

Bending to the microphone – which had been set low for the diminutive Saiki - Chappell stumbled through the Bantu words she'd learned for the occasion. Jack had a transcript somewhere, but it didn't matter what she said. All that mattered was the roar of approval from the crowd when she cut the ribbon.

As Alex, the president and the rest of the dignitaries waved, fireworks erupted from behind the visitor centre. The crowd roared again. It should have been weird seeing the rockets explode in the full glare of the sun – Jack's idea of fireworks was New Year's Eve on the Embankment, watching the London Eye go nova. But somehow it worked. Like everything African, rockets in the sun turned everything you knew on its head and made it beautiful all over again.

He wrote that down before he forgot it. It really was too much for the piece he was writing for *The Times*, but he'd find a space for it somewhere. Maybe the half-finished novel under his bed.

He sneezed. Then he sneezed again. Typical – the UK hay fever season was over but the pollen had followed him out here. Or maybe he'd just developed an allergy to Africa. Either way, something was telling him it was time to go home.

While the rest of the press hurried from the grandstand to follow the bigwigs on their tour, Jack held back. A man had just separated himself from the rest of the official group and was kneeling at the front of the stage, waving at someone in the crowd. It was Paul Malamba.

As Jack watched, an enormous woman pushed forward from the crowd, followed by three lanky children. The eldest was a girl; the younger two were boys. The boys looked about the same age as Jack's kids, who were currently in Florida with their Uncle Henry. Malamba pointed out a set of steps; minutes later, his family had joined him on the stage.

He embraced his wife and together they followed their president into the visitor centre.

The fireworks continued to explode against the vast bowl of the sky. In the distance, the waterfall cascaded down the plateau wall while, deep underground, the future of the Republic of Limpopo awaited.

This Large Print Book, for people
who cannot read normal print,
is published under the auspices of

THE ULVERSCROFT FOUNDATION